I0614190

Social Studies
Book One

Dying to be Popular
plus eleven
An anthology of Short Stories
focused on Social Issues
Audrey Austin

SOCIAL STUDIES

Book One – Dying To Be Popular Plus Eleven

Also for your reading pleasure:

**Book Two – Shattered and Beaten Plus Eleven –
ISBN 978-0-9780238-9-8**

**Book Three – Weaving Alice Plus Eleven – ISBN 978-
0-9937163-0-0**

A Trilogy of Anthologies

Short Stories

Which keep the focus on Social Issues

Written and compiled by

Audrey Austin

SOCIAL STUDIES

This is Book One of a trilogy of anthologies containing short stories focused on Social Issues.

Cover design by Susan Ruby K.; Yuneekpix.com

ISBN 978-0-9780238-8-1

Other Books by Audrey Austin

Sara, a Canadian Saga

The Silent Star Plus a Dozen

Reawakening

Keeping It Simple

Ellen and The Hummingtree

Moose Road – a Canadian Tragedy

Beyond The Blue

Recompense

When God Gives Us Spring

Social Studies - a Trilogy - Books 1, 2 and 3

TABLE OF CONTENTS

DYING TO BE POPULAR

I lay, a massive mound upon the mattress. I
stare with dreams at the purple picture frame atop the
lace fringed runner atop my bedroom dresser. Within
the frame I see my mother; petite, cute, laughing; my
father tall, stern but with a boyish crinkle around his
soft brown eyes. I'm there in the middle; angry, broken
and just plain tired; tired of being me; tired of
pretending that I don't give one damn what others
think; sick and tired of being *the fat girl in 10C.*

Today is my fifteenth birthday. Mom has
planned a backyard barbecue party for me. It will be
burgers, hotdogs and birthday cake with ice cream for
dessert. I've invited six kids to come along to my
party, all girls. A boy wouldn't be caught dead at my

6

party. I'm not even sure the girls will show up.
Friendship is something that eludes me.

"Sandra, for the tenth time, get out of bed!
Your breakfast is getting cold and if you don't get a
move on, you'll be late for school again!"

"I'm coming, Ma. I'm coming."

I don't want to get out of bed. I don't want to
eat breakfast. I don't want to go to school. I know my
choices are limited and what I do want is buried
somewhere beneath the burgers, the cokes, the poutine,
the pizzas. Food is my drug of choice. Where food
leads, I follow. I remember I used to have dreams. I've
forgotten what they were. There are so many things I
don't want that I can't remember what I do want.
Desire is lost, hidden, and impossible.

It's not as easy to roll out of bed as it used to be
but I make the effort and feel the bedroom carpet's

warmth beneath my feet. I sit on the bed's edge while I think about what I will wear to school. I really do have some beautiful clothing, good quality and a cut above the Wal Mart synthetic crap that most of the girls in school wear. I'd give my right arm to be able to dress like the other girls in school with their tight-ass jeans and cute, colourful, bare midriff tops but there is nothing tight about a size 20 rear-end and the only thing below my bountiful boobs is fat. I don't have a waist. Mom takes me shopping at Pennington's where all the fat, old ladies buy their clothes. She spends a fortune on me and looks for gratitude.

I open my closet door and choose the light green long-sleeved tent top that hides a multitude of sins. I decide to wear the denim slacks with the elastic waist. Wearing these clothes I stand in front of my full-length mirror. I'm not pleased with what I see but I know it's as good as it's going to get. And what's the difference anyway? It's not as though people notice what a fat person wears. No one takes the time to see past the fat.

As I continue to stare at the fat girl in the mirror I remember that until the age of seven I was an average sized kid. It was shortly after my seventh birthday when Mom joined a bridge club. She would get together with her friends once a week to play cards on a Wednesday evening. On these nights my Daddy would be charged with getting me to bed. He would sit beside me as I rested my sleepy head against the pillow and he would read me my bed-time story.

I loved these times with my Daddy and I came to look forward to the nights when Mom wasn't there to help me with my bath and bedtime routine. While he read, Daddy would softly caress my arm. I enjoyed it. I felt very safe and protected.

But it happened one night that he began to caress me in a different kind of way and in different sorts of places. I wasn't sure what to think of this but Daddy assured me this is what Daddies do to express their affection to their beautiful little girls. "We don't need to tell Mommy," he said.

I didn't tell Mom anything but by the time I was ten years old I knew that what Daddy was doing was wrong. I felt ashamed.

"Daddy, I don't want you to touch me anymore," I told him one night as he was sitting beside me on my bed. But he didn't stop.

I knew I had to find a way to make him stop. It was around that time that I began to bury my shame with French-fries, donuts and after-school hamburgers and cokes. By the time I was thirteen I was wearing a size eighteen and my Daddy had lost interest in me. He didn't comment on my weight gain. "I guess you are getting too grown-up for bedtime stories," is all he ever said to me.

My mother's impatience brings me back to the present as she shouts, "Sandra, I am not going to call you again!"

"Okay, Ma. I'm just about ready."

I tuck my childhood memories away, slip my feet into my size seven Birkenstocks and leave the safety of my bedroom to join my parents in the kitchen at the breakfast table.

"Good morning, Princess." Daddy raises his eyes and peers at me from behind the huge expanse of the morning newspaper. "That's a pretty top you're wearing, birthday girl!"

"Thank-you, Daddy."

His attention returns to the paper.

"Sit down, Sandra. If we don't hurry up you'll be late for school and I'll be late for work," she scolds as she slides the buttermilk pancakes onto my plate.

Just as I am reaching for the Maple Syrup Daddy folds his paper, pushes his chair back from the table and announces, "Ladies, it has been a pleasure. I'm off to work now. He gives Mom a kiss on the cheek, sends me a quick wink, picks up his briefcase from the side table and I sit there staring at my food as I listen to the hum of his car as it backs out of our suburban driveway.

"Don't play with your food, Sandra," Mom snaps.

I smother my plate with Maple syrup and dig into the pancakes. They are delicious and now that I've had my morning fix I feel a little better until Mom says,

"If you don't get a move on you're going to miss the school bus."

So ends my moment of comfort. Daddy has promised me a car of my own for my sixteenth birthday but that's a year away. The thought of travelling on the school bus only serves to make me want to go back to bed. "Can't you drop me off at school this morning, Ma?"

"Sandra, you know that is out of the question! I have a good forty minute drive ahead of me to get to work and it's in the opposite direction of your school. Maybe if you didn't operate in slow motion every morning we could be ready to leave the house earlier. Then maybe I could give you a drive."

I eat all my pancakes. I munch on a handful of green grapes. I drink a glass of orange juice and slowly slurp a mug of coffee. "Will Daddy be here for my party after school, Ma?"

"He will be if he can be, Sandra."

"What time will you be home?"

"Don't worry, Sandra. I'm going to pick up your cake from the bakery on my way home from work and I'll be here in plenty of time to start the barbecuing before your friends arrive." Mom smiles her pretty petite smile. She walks over to where I'm sitting and bends to give me a hug. She thinks I don't notice that her little arms don't even stretch long enough to get around half my body. She pats my head like I would pet a dog. "Have a good day at school, dear. I have to go now or I'll be late," she says. "Be sure you lock the door when you leave and get a move on or you really will miss your bus."

And she is gone.

And I am alone.

I know I don't have much time but I get up from the table, take a couple slices of bread out of the breadbox and slip them into the toaster. Once the bread pops up I slather it with strawberry jam, eat it quickly before I manipulate my body to get the knapsack onto my back. I'm as ready as I will ever be to face another day.

I walk the half block to the bus stop. I keep my distance from the two boys, Eddie and Jerry, who are standing there waiting for the bus.

"I remember her when she had only one belly," Eddie snickered.

"Yeah," Jerry laughed, "Sandra's so fat she's taller sideways!"

I've known these kids since kindergarten. I pretend I don't hear them. I pretend I don't care.

The bus arrives. It's the usual crowd; the same kids I've been travelling with to high school for the past two years. I make my way down the aisle to the back seat. This is a practice I initiated after my first time taking this school bus. I made a big mistake on my first day of school. I took a window seat and all the way to school I had to hear the kids making a big joke out of the fact that there was no room for anyone to sit down beside me. I was just thirteen and I overheard one of the older girls say, "She's a truck. She's so fat that her beeper goes off when she's backing up!" Everybody laughs.

I want to disappear. I want to die. So starts my high school misery.

After two years of hearing all these jokes about me and insults thrown at me you would think I'd get used to it and not pay these kids any mind. But the hurt never goes away. Every nasty slur is a knife in my hurting heart.

At last the school bus pulls into the school parking lot. I make my way into the building and to my first class. I've known the kids in my home room for most of my life. Some of them used to be my friends but once I started to put on the pounds they began finding reasons why they didn't want to spend time with me. A couple of the girls to whom I had dared to give birthday party invitations did greet me with a smile. In unison they said, "Happy birthday, Sandra!"

"Thanks," I replied. They are the only two who acknowledged my birthday. The rest of the skinny bitches ignored me as usual.

I took my usual place in class. I overheard one of the boys in the back of the room laughingly say, "Somebody should buy her bathroom scales for her birthday!"

"Ha!" I heard his friend reply, "She's so fat when she steps on the scale it says to be continued."

I listened to all the dirty giggles and laughter. I was grateful when our teacher, Miss MacIntosh, came into the classroom. And so the morning passed.

At lunch time I bought a small salad and ate it as I sat alone in the school cafeteria. I deliberately ordered this kind of small salad every day at school. I was embarrassed to allow anyone to see me eating more than this. Once I finished my salad I walked two blocks away from the school to Tim Hortons where I bought the donuts. This day I took the long way back to school for the afternoon session, stopping first at McDonalds

where I bought a Big Mac and an order of fries.
Sometimes I'd go to the Dairy Queen too and get
myself a sundae or a banana split but today I passed on
the ice cream. I knew I'd have ice cream with my
birthday cake after school.

I always feel good when I'm eating the food but
when it's all eaten I feel the familiar weight of shame;
the same kind of shame I felt when I was little and
Daddy was reading me a bedtime story.

And so the school day passes. I face the fire and
submit myself to humiliation once again on the bus ride
home. I sit as usual on the back seat, alone. As usual
Eddie and Jerry were on the same bus. When I reached
my bus stop they followed me off the bus as usual.
Eddie never runs out of jokes. He is inherently mean.
To Jerry he says, "Hey Jerry, Sandra's so fat she has
her own postal code!"

As usual I pretend I don't hear them. As usual I
am relieved when they turn the corner and no longer
follow me on the sidewalk.

By the time I get home from school I find my
Mom out in the backyard. I see she has decorated the
patio table and hung balloons from the pergola. She
has the hamburgers and hotdogs on the grill. I see the
relish, mustard, chopped onions and buns on the table
beside the gas barbecue. I see a large gift-wrapped
box topped with a big pink ribbon bow in the centre of
the patio table. The gift is surrounded by six happy
birthday paper plates and colourful napkins. She has
worked hard and the backyard is pretty and party-ready.

Mom greets me when I enter the backyard. "Hi
sweetheart! I see you are on your own. What time are
your friends coming? Maybe I've got these things on
the grill too soon?"

"I don't know, Ma. Maybe they've gone home to change before they come. I think I'll do the same."

I go into the house, make my way to my room, and sit down once again on my bed. I want to cry but tears seem as senseless and useless as I feel. Except for the two girls who said happy birthday early this morning no one has said a word to me and not one of the six girls I invited said anything about my party. I change into a lounging dress better described as a tent. From my shoulders its blueness hangs loosely down until it barely touches my toes. I like to hide in my clothes. I have nowhere else to hide.

Back out into the backyard Mom asks me again, "What time do you expect your friends to arrive, dear? These burgers are just about ready to eat."

"I don't know, Ma. Is Daddy coming home for my party?"

"No, Sandra. He's tied up at work. You will see him later tonight."

I walk across the patio, sit down in one of Ma's garden chairs and wait. After twenty minutes pass Mom comes and sits down beside me. After another half-hour passes I say, "Nobody's coming, Ma."

I try not to notice her tears. I know Mom feels sorry for me.

"We'll party together," she says.

Ma and me, we sit at the patio table and eat hamburgers. Mom lights the candles on my cake and her solo performance of *happy birthday, dear Sandra* is pretty pathetic but I pretend I'm enjoying myself.

After we eat I open my birthday present. The big box contains a smaller box which contains a little box which contains a tiny box which, when opened, reveals a very beautiful ruby ring. The ruby is my birthstone. The little card is signed. It says love from Mommy and Daddy. I recognize the handwriting as my mother's. I know Daddy had nothing to do with its acquisition.

I don't know what I feel. My feelings are buried beneath too many layers of secrets, shame, fear and disappointment.

Mom does her best to give me a happy memory. Ma loves me. I know my mother loves me.

After our party I leave my Mom to put away the food and tidy up the backyard. I go into the bathroom, fill the tub with warm water. I remove my clothes before I remove the razor blade from the medicine cabinet. I get into the bathtub. I feel the calming warmth. I touch the ring, the ruby red brilliance of my mother's love. I hope by being in the bathtub that what

I am about to do will not mess up Ma's pretty bathroom

too much. It is well that my secret will die with me.

DANIEL'S DESTINY

Daniel was homeless but there was something about him that separated him from the many who, like himself, sought and found a safe hide-away to sleep throughout the day; who wandered the dark downtown streets and alleys pillaging the garbage cans at night to keep body and soul alive. The light within that kept Daniel apart from the others was something called faith. Collective failure may be what brought him into this sad state of affairs but it would be individual insight and initiative that would carry him out of his pitiful plight and place him once more onto a productive path. His remembrance of Alice's good advice was a godsend.

He had lived with her for 12 years. He adored Alice. When the business of work or other necessary activities of life kept them apart he thought only of her. He yearned for the time when they would be together again.

And Alice loved Daniel like she had loved no other. He was her first and she told everyone he would be her last. She poured her affection onto him. Together they shared unconditional love; something Alice had never been able to achieve with another human being. Always she whispered encouragement and praise into his ear and Daniel responded with loyalty and affection.

Both Alice and Daniel felt secure in their love for one another.

When Alice became ill everything changed. Daniel was not with her when she sat that life-changing day on a chair in Dr. Finnamore's office. "Alice," he said, "the cancer is spreading in spite of the treatments you are receiving. I'm sorry to tell you that there is not much more that the medical profession can do for you."

"How much time do I have, Doctor?"

"Only God knows the answer to your question, Alice, but I would ballpark a period of three to six months. I'm very sorry."

A tearful Alice returned home that day. Her concern was not for herself. Her heart broke thinking of her Daniel being left alone. She determined to find him a new home but she was not optimistic. They had spent twelve years together and there were not many who wanted to take in a 12 year old Jack Russell Terrier. Families wanted puppies.

Alice had no relative willing and able to step up to the plate. She had no friend who would adopt Daniel. Nobody wanted an old dog, especially one as pampered as Daniel. Of this Alice was well aware.

In the area where Alice lived there used to be a no-kill animal shelter. At that time loving pet owners felt the assurance that, should anything happen making them unable to continue to care for their pet, there was a safe harbour where the animals could reside. There they could have at least their basic needs met. Some animals, especially the younger ones, were often fortunate enough to meet a person willing to open the door and invite the grateful dog or cat into their family. These animals were often blessed to find a forever home.

Alice knew that Daniel would not be so blessed.

The economy suffered in the part of the world where Alice lived. Governments federal, provincial and municipal spent most of their time finding ways to provide what they called *cut-backs*.

Just like the old adage that says, *"while the rich get richer, the poor get poorer,"* those who suffered the most from the cut-backs were ordinary hard-working people who lost full time jobs and therefore could no longer provide for their families with the without-benefits, part-time jobs that were on the increase; recipients of welfare who were primarily single mothers who had no one to care for their children if they did try to find one of the elusive part-time jobs; the children because spending on education decreased and classroom sizes increased as a result of teacher lay-offs; the children again because after-school sports and cultural programmes were dropped and children returned to empty apartments and homes or wandered the streets aimlessly after school finding trouble that seemed to lurk in a sad society that made money from the sale to kids of drugs and alcohol; the seniors who were informed they must continue to work in the business or industrial environment until they were sixty-seven when everyone knew employers didn't want the old people on their staff and there was always the unlikelihood, if you were let go, of being hired anywhere if you were over the age of forty, not to mention the additional fear that the age limit may soon be raised to seventy; the mentally, emotionally and physically challenged whose disability cheques were diminished and of course, the innocent, trusting, defenseless animals who were at the very bottom of the hurting, crowded barrel. Homeless pets suffered because heartless government officials declared they could no longer find their way to support the no-kill shelters.

No, Alice did not fear for her own future. Her spiritual stability gave her the assurance that she would find peace in her passing from this tired, corrupt and broken world.

Alice knew that Daniel's opportunity for adoption was a very narrow one indeed and she could not bear to think, even for one second, that her beloved pet would be murdered. She could not consider the animal shelter an option for the gift God had placed in her charge.

Each evening she would sit with him and, in spite of her own increasing unbearable pain, she did everything possible to take care of Daniel's physical needs. She kept him warm and fed. Because of her illness Alice could no longer work outside the home. She needed to rely upon welfare which had also suffered government cut-backs. Though she could not financially afford it, when she was no longer strong enough to walk with him outside, she hired a young student to give him his daily exercise. Sometimes she would go with little or no food herself in order to keep Daniel well fed. She tried in every imaginable way to find someone to offer her life companion a home but it was to no avail. Time passed all too quickly. Alice's physical pain now matched her emotional anguish. She did not fear death but she still could not bring herself to surrender Daniel to an uncaring shelter world where he would be murdered before his time.

Like a slap in the face, the day arrived when she had to make a choice. After much thought and prayer the difficult decision she reached was to give Daniel his freedom. Before opening the front door she spent a very long time talking to him; explaining the atrocities that some humans might inflict upon him. She talked to him about staying out of sight as much as possible throughout the day and to do his foraging under the safety of the moon's glow. She advised him not to bark loud or to do any damage that would cause him to be picked up and taken to the animal shelter where, if no one claimed him within three days, he would be executed even though he had committed no crime.

Daniel cocked his head to one side as he always did when listening to his mistress. His deep brown eyes became watery but remained lucid. Alice knew that her clever Daniel understood all that was being said. Daniel demonstrated his ability to think clearly even throughout the periods of confusion that overwhelmed him when he knew his owner was suffering. He sat cuddled on her lap and licked her tear-soaked face. He spoke to her in the only language he possessed which was that of his body.

"I know, Daniel," Alice responded. "Don't cry my boy," she said in response to his whimpering plea.

As it happens it was just a few hours before Alice's death when she opened the front door of her house and bid farewell to the small but smart terrier.

Daniel did not run. He walked with dignity through the doorway, out onto the verandah, across the patio and onto the driveway that led him to the road which he crossed alone for the very first time. For just a few seconds he hesitated there on the sidewalk. Again he cocked his head to one side and looked back at Alice who stood in the doorway. It was as though he were asking, "Are you sure?"

"Go, boy!" Alice ordered. "God be with you, my dear little fellow."

Daniel still did not run. It was a warm sunny day and he proceeded along the sidewalk as though he were out for a Sunday stroll. There were no people about and he walked and he walked until he came across a busy city street with traffic lights; something he had never seen before. Always Alice had walked him in the park or through the streets of his quiet residential neighbourhood.

The large number of noisy, polluting vehicles frightened him. Daniel had no road sense and he had not the slightest idea what he was to do or where he was to go. He turned to go back home but quickly sensed something which made him realize that returning to the loving Alice was not one of his options. He continued his walk into unknown territory.

He was becoming tired by the time he found his way into an alley which ran for several blocks behind some stores and other commercial buildings. There he met up with a couple of other dogs and more than a few cats who seemed to be eking out an existence from the garbage cans that lined one side of the long alley.

Daniel had never seen a cat before. He drew close to a little ginger-coloured one. *Hiss! Hiss!* One little long-nailed paw cut into his side. He started to lick at his wound. *Meow! Hiss!* The cats' screeching terrified him and caused him to run faster than his little twelve year old heart could comfortably handle.

Heart racing he slowed his pace. He cocked his leg to relieve himself and once he had done that a large dog approached sniffing and softly growling. The big fellow also lifted his leg and peed atop Daniel's contribution. Daniel understood this meant that the big dog was more dominant than himself. Daniel had always been one of a more submissive and passive nature. Now he wondered if this was something he would need to consider changing.

Although the strange animal was much bigger than Daniel, he did not appear to be threatening in any way such as the nervous, hungry cats had been. Fortunately Daniel's wound was not severe and already the blood was beginning to coagulate. He decided he would refrain from licking it. Instead he would leave well enough alone.

Daniel knew nothing of dog breeds. He didn't know that this large creature was a German Shepherd. What he did recognize was that this was a dog; a dog, though larger, not very different from himself. He allowed the big dog to enjoy his sniffing and he didn't object when the big fellow wanted to sidle up against him. In fact he rather enjoyed the warmth and the sidling reminded him of the petting he had often received with pleasure from his mistress.

The big dog barked and maneuvered playfully as he moved away from Daniel, treading further down the alley. Daniel didn't hesitate for long. Indeed, he fancied the company and, short tail wagging; he accepted the Shepherd's invitation to follow.

The German Shepherd led Daniel into a narrow walk-way which ran between two faded brick buildings. This small space was protected from the elements by the high walls on either side which were topped by roof overhangs which kept the walk-way dry in the most inclement weather and at the front there was a large commercial sign which prevented anyone from entering the walk-way from the city street. The only small opening was off the alley. It was the home of the German Shepherd. Daniel discovered that this home was shared by a sensible, shiny black Lab, a long, short-legged but very affectionate Beagle and a placid Collie dog with pointed nose and long, thick hair.

Daniel could not believe his good fortune. He was welcomed by the other dogs. Some might say these animals were homeless but Daniel was a smart Jack Russell and he recognized that this walk-way could be and would be his new home.

By following his room mates' example Daniel learned in no time at all to forage in the garbage cans behind the city shops. He learned how to climb along the ledge of a fence to the top of the big, blue dumpster behind the Fairview Restaurant. Just like his friends he

found meat-covered bones and often delicious morsels

of steak, roast beef, fish and chicken. He had watched

how his new brothers and sisters foraged and he learned

to carry the food in his mouth back to their shared home

in the walk-way.

In his new world Daniel learned many lessons

but the one he valued most was the knowledge that dog

was dog's best friend. He was unaware that Alice

looked down from above. She was grateful that she had

made the right decision and not left his fate in the hands

of uncaring humans who no longer provided no-kill

shelters for unwanted or homeless animals. Daniel

missed Alice and her caring ways but he learned to love

his new family. They had sought and found a safe hide-

away and they were smart enough to sleep throughout

the day. They pillaged the dumpster and the garbage

cans at night and in this way they helped each other to keep body and soul alive.

The light within, the faith, that kept Daniel apart from the others was the same thing that kept him and his new friends together. They had faith in themselves and faith in each other. They helped each other and in this way they made a decent life for themselves. It wasn't always easy but they were clever dogs. The smallest of the lot, Daniel walked tall.

QUEST FOR CAMMIRAND

Peter Lowenza loved his job. As an insurance investigator for one of the largest insurance companies in Canada he was well travelled and well paid. He lived usually happily with his wife, Louise, in an upscale Toronto neighborhood. Their luxurious home had an equally big mortgage. Peter was up for promotion. He wanted this promotion so much he could taste it. He would put the money that came with it to good use. Once they felt more financially secure Peter and Louise hoped to start a family. Whether or not he would receive the raise hinged heavily on the outcome of the case he was currently handling. The beneficiary of a life policy held by his company was coined whereabouts unknown. It was Peter's job to find her. He was determined to locate the young woman with the strange name of Cammirand Gauthier even if it did take him straight into Central Ontario's black bear wilderness.

He didn't know a lot about her but he did know that Cammirand was born in the small mining town of Elliot Lake, Ontario twenty-five years earlier. She was the daughter of a miner who, along with his wife, was tragically killed in an auto accident leaving Cammirand an orphan at the age of seventeen. An intelligent girl she worked hard and graduated from Laurentian University with a Bachelor's degree in health sciences. She planned a career in nursing but these plans were cut short when she met and married Jessie Gauthier.

Peter's file on the deceased Jessie Gauthier told him that Cammirand had married a man twenty years her senior. President of one of the largest corporations in Ontario Jessie was known in the business community as an aggressive, often ruthless, businessman who would stop at nothing to achieve his goals. At the early age of forty-five Jessie suffered a massive coronary leaving Cammirand a wealthy widow. There was perfunctory attendance at the funeral home. Peter was advised by his superior who attended the service that no tears were shed that day.

According to Peter's records Cammirand left the marital home after only two years of marriage which meant five years ago. He had no clues to go on. He had no idea where in the world she could be but he decided to start his quest in her home town in the hope that he could find people who may have some idea as to her whereabouts.

Peter had been given a photo which clearly showed her to be an attractive blond girl with a contagious smile. Yet Peter detected something in the eyes that told him this young woman's life wasn't the typical Cinderella story one expected to hear given the young woman's working class background and her subsequent marriage into one of Canada's most wealthy families. Was Jessie Gauthier's aggressiveness something he took home from the office? Is this why Cammirand left the grandiose waterfront estate and a most desirable life of luxury with nothing more than a few dollars and a suitcase filled with essential clothing?

Peter pulled his Mercedes into the parking lot of the decaying motel on Highway 108 in Elliot Lake. Beside the Chevy trucks his vehicle stood out like a diamond in a coal bin. He had done his research and knew the Bonny Vu's history. He made his first stop there thinking that it was a good possibility Cammirand may have taken a room there. At the time she left home Jessie hired detectives who undertook a massive search to no avail. From the records he learned Cammirand never used any credit cards, never withdrew from joint accounts. She definitely didn't want to be found by Jessie Gauthier.

Knowing she was not wanting to do anything traceable, Peter hoped he was correct in his assessment of the situation she was in when and, indeed, if she headed for her home town.

Getting out of the car Peter stood on the cracked pavement of the parking lot in front of the shabby inn owned by Gus and Bonny Arnone. He had read it was once a fine establishment. The Chianti bottles and red checkered table cloths had adorned the once most popular dining room in town but that was many years ago when its owners were young and optimistic about their future. Today the building was scheduled for demolition to make way for a brand new supermarket.

Peter found the Arnones in the office. An elderly couple they were aging a little more gracefully than their physical surroundings. Holding up the photo of Cammirand he asked the all important question. "Do you recognize this young woman?"

"Cammy? Sure, I remember Cammy." Gus answered without hesitation. "Who wouldn't remember her? She told us her real name is Cammirand, funny name we thought, but we called her Cammy. A pretty woman, maybe 25 tops. She told me she came here for some peace and quiet but we knew she came here to hide," Gus revealed. "She tried but she couldn't fool us."

He was warming up to his story, happy to share his memories of the girl who reminded him of his own grand-daughter. They had often wondered what had happened to Cammy. "She was a quiet guest. All guests should be so quiet but doncha know we are not usually that fortunate. Some of the rowdy lot we get these days are enough to make your head spin. They make too much noise for me and I'm half deaf. But, Cammy, she was a quiet girl. At first she kept pretty much to herself. But I do remember one incident that happened soon after her arrival. It was maybe a day or so after she checked in. It was a hot night and as you can tell we have no air conditioning here," he said picking up the guest register and fanning himself with it.

"I recall she was sitting on the step outside her room trying to cool off that evening when that guy just pulled up out of nowhere in his truck. Like a shot he bent down on one knee and took her picture. That must have been seven or eight years ago. It was the oddest thing. He seemed to appear out of nowhere and as fast as he came he was back in the truck and gone. I saw it happen through this window." Age had a way of making Gus's vision a liar and his aging memory always confirmed his vision. Bonny, ten years younger than his salty seventy-six, didn't let him get away with much. Quiet up to now she decided it was her turn to jump into the telling of the story.

"It wasn't seven or eight years ago. It was five years ago, Gus, almost to the day. I remember it clear as a bell." Bonny interrupted. "But why are you rattling on about Cammy when you don't even know who you're talking to?" Not mincing her words she demanded, "Who are you and what is your interest in Cammy?"

"Sorry, ma'am, let me introduce myself to you kind folks. My name is Peter Lowenza. I'm an investigator working with the Moon Life Insurance Company. Cammirand's husband, Jessie Gauthier, died a couple of weeks ago in Sudbury. Jessie and Cammirand were separated but Jessie never changed the beneficiary in his Will. She stands to inherit millions from his estate; that is if I can locate her.

"Millions! That sure is one gargantuan amount of money! Why it never occurred to me that Cammy came from money. For sure we don't get many with money at the Bonny Vu anymore. Like I said that evening I could see her from the office window here. She was sitting on the cement step outside her room. The guy flashed his picture then raced back to his truck. But that wasn't the end of it. Cammy got up and chased the guy. I could see she was mad as a hornet's nest.   She was shaking her hands in the air after him. But you know even in this big upset I could see she was a few steps up from the riff-raff who pay by the month here these days. She was a fine young woman but I sure didn't get any impression she was rich."

"You ought to know having a rich husband doesn't necessarily make a woman rich, Gus!" Bonny interrupted again, this time with straight mouth anger. "I could tell you a thing or two, Mister."

"Please do, Madam", Peter encouraged.

"Well, I don't like to get involved in people's problems as a rule but, Cammy; she was kind of special to me. Like Gus said she was the age of my grand-daughter. I tried to keep my eye on her while she was staying here. Sure, when she first arrived she was quiet and kept to herself but I'd chat with her each day when I'd visit her room to bring clean towels. I invited her and during the two weeks she stayed here she came over a few times to have supper with me and Gus. We're Italian, you know. Cammy told me she loved Italian food. I make the best spaghetti and meatballs in town if I do say so myself. You can take my word for it, Cammy loved spaghetti and meatballs.

Once Cammy got to know me a little better she confided in me. She told me her husband was a no-good bum. Did you know he sent her to hospital more than once? Of course Cammy told me she never let on to the doctors what really happened to her. She would tell the doctor she fell on the ice or she bumped into a door.

Now don't get me wrong, she wasn't trying to protect

that no good son of a you know what. She told me she

had to lie to protect herself. He told her that if she ever

told anyone what really went on behind closed doors he

would kill her. She said she thought often about

leaving but he had told her she would never get away.

He would follow her to the ends of the earth and he

would find her. I tell you he was a bum. I don't give a

rat's tail how many millions he had. The poor kid was

only eighteen when she met this monster. She said he

wined her, dined her, and made her feel like a princess.

Cammy was an orphan. Did you know that?

She worked hard to support herself and to get herself

through university. She wasn't used to the rich life

Jessie was offering her. She thought he was just too

good to be true. All the time she dated him he could do

no wrong. She told me he sent her flowers, bought her expensive gifts.

But that princess treatment ended in a hurry once Cammy said I do. Marriage to Jessie changed everything. Once he married her Jessie figured he owned her. She was his possession. He could do whatever he wanted and what he wanted was to use and abuse that poor girl. For seven years Cammy was under his thumb. He controlled her every move. Whenever he decided he didn't like what she was doing he would beat her senseless. He was a smart character though, always making sure the bruises were hidden under her clothing. The poor girl tried to make a marriage with that tyrant but there's a limit to what any poor soul can tolerate in this world."

"You're saying Jessie Gauthier was a wife-beater?" Peter asked.

"Don't you doubt my wife!" Gus jumped in. "If Bonny tells you something you know it's God's truth. Besides I know a little about this myself. When Cammy first signed up for her room I noticed what a pretty blond girl she was. I may be old but I'm not blind and I haven't lost my liking for young blonds. But that evening when she was sitting out there on that step her hair was as dark brown as mine used to be," he said rubbing his balding pate. "She used some kind of dye to change that colour. I know she was running scared."

Bonny jumped in with, "That's right, Gus. She was running scared. What woman in her right mind wouldn't be scared knowing that her husband had every intention of carrying through on his threats? For all her fear she was very brave. She prayed for the strength to get away and somewhere deep inside herself she finally found the courage she needed. But the sad part of the story is she had nowhere to go, no family to run home to. She came here to Elliot Lake, the only home she had ever known, but with no family or friends here she knew she had to move on, especially after that day the man jumped out of his truck to take her picture. Cammy knew the guy had been hired by Jessie to find her."

"Did she give you any indication of where she was going when she left here?"

Bonny grew thoughtful before she answered. "Well, Cammy was here for only two weeks. She didn't say where she was heading. She did mention that she had a couple of cousins in The Sault but no close family to speak of. She talked a little bit about one of her school chums from Sudbury who she thought was living in Spanish with her brother who runs some kind of campground there. Elizabeth I think the girl's name was. Can't remember the last name. I often wondered if she headed to Spanish to be near her friend but I couldn't say for sure."

"Spanish, you say? Well, thank you good folks for your time. You've been most helpful."

"No problem," Gus said. "I hope you find her."

"She will be relieved to know that creep of a husband is out of her life for good now," Bonny added. "I don't like to speak ill of the dead but the world is a better place since Jessie Gauthier left it. Maybe now the poor girl can stop running and make a good life for herself. When you find her give her a hug from old Bonny."

"I'll do that, yes, ma'am. Here's my card. You hold on to it and if you think of anything else that may help me find her please don't hesitate to give me a call. Have a good day now."

Mr. Lowenza climbed back into his vehicle. Gus and Bonny watched the silver Mercedes roll out of their parking lot onto Highway 108. "Nice car," Gus said with envy.

"Never mind no nice cars," Bonny retorted. "We've got work to get done."

Driving south on 108 Peter made a left turn onto Highway 17. The drive up from Toronto had been stressful with too much traffic on Highway 69. By the time he arrived in Spanish he felt tired and decided to call it a day. When he spotted Vance's Motor Inn on his left he decided to stop for a meal and a good night's sleep. He would start checking out all the campground sites in the morning. He knew there must be a lot of them in this neck of the woods.

At daybreak Peter was awake, alert and in no mood to be wasting time. After a quick breakfast in

Vance's Restaurant he jumped into his vehicle and headed east on Highway 17. Minutes later he spotted a road sign which simply read Camp Grounds. Turning the wheel he made a sharp right onto a narrow, dusty dirt road.

Approaching the park he could see it was more run down and neglected than the Bonny Vu had been. Still there were a few old trailers hunkered down beside the pretty small lake. Everything he viewed had seen better days. He parked the car on a grassy knoll beside the gravelly drive that led to a ramshackle building. Looking at his silver Mercedes he wondered how long he would need to drive to find a car wash. His car was wearing the dirt road.

Peter sighed. Turning his head away from the dust covered car toward what he guessed was the campground office he had to smile when he read the sign above the door. It read "Heavenly Haven" proudly contradicting what was clearly evident to anyone who cared to notice. Peter Lowenza noticed but in his line of work nothing much in life surprised him anymore.

Upon opening the tired screen door a little bell chimed bringing a middle-aged, short, rotund, red faced gentleman from a back room to the front desk.

Extending his arm to shake hands Peter's eyes did a swift survey of the room and its occupant. No sight for sore eyes, he thought but he said, "Good morning, sir." Handing over his business card he wasted no time getting down to business. "Are you the owner of this fine establishment?"

"What's it to ya?" was the response.

"I'm looking for a young woman named Cammirand Gauthier and ....

The short fat man took in the silk suit, the sharp leather shoes and interrupting Peter mid sentence his jealousy snarled, "Don't know nuthin, don't care nuthin."

Not even slightly put off by the rude response Peter calmly stated, "First of all, I need to know who I'm talking to. I'm not here to waste my time or yours. Are you the owner of this camp?"

Unused to people standing up to him the fellow recognized the authority in the investigator's voice. Since as a teenager he had spent his first stint in jail for stealing cars he was afraid of authority. His fear made the decision to back down and go along with whatever the guy had in mind. The quicker the city slicker was off his land the better he'd like it. "I'm Gordie Karlin. I'm the owner of this place. I don't know nuthin about no Cammy Gauthier."

Not missing a trick Peter smiled knowing he was first time lucky. "But you know people called her Cammy, eh? How did you happen to know that if you don't know anything about her? When was she here?"

"Oh, geez! All right, so she was here. It's a long time ago, gotta be five or six years ago. Came looking for my sister Liz."

"So tell me what happened, Gordie. Best to tell me now, eh? We don't want to bring in the police do we? "His subtle threat produced the hoped for result.

"Police? Are you crazy? I don't want no cops around here. I got enough trouble. Geez, I told you I don't know nuthin. She came here looking for Liz. She was Liz's friend, nothing to do with me. When she came looking for Liz I did what I always do, kept my nose out of other people's business."

"So tell me what happened, Gordie," Peter persisted.

"I don't know who did it, I swear to God. I didn't know a darn thing about it until Liz came and said she was leaving with Cammy."

"Tell me what happened, Gordie," Peter repeated.

"Okay, okay, but I'm telling you I don't know nuthin. Cammy had only been here about a week or so. She was staying with Liz in her trailer. Liz comes running here one night telling me two guys jumped Cammy when she was walking back to the trailer from the outhouse. I don't know who they were. Honest to God I don't know nuthin. The girl was pretty beat up. She was crying to beat the band and Liz tells me she was raped by those guys."

"Did you report this to the police? Was Cammirand taken to hospital? Tell me what happened, Gordie."

"I'm telling you all I know and it aint much. No, Cammy didn't want no cops brought into it. She was running from her husband. At least that's what Liz told me. I figured these guys were hired by Jessie to teach her a hard lesson," Gordie said summing up his story. "That's all I know. I don't know nuthin. After that night Liz and Cammy both packed up and headed out of here. That's five years ago. I haven't seen or heard from either one of them since. Liz took off just like that and left me here alone holding the bag."

"You sound pretty bitter, Gordie," Peter suggested.

"Bitter?" Gordie's sardonic laugh held the answer in its grasp. "Who wouldn't be bitter?

Wouldn't you be if it happened to you? Some sister! Took off just like that leaving me here with no help whatsoever to run this godforsaken camp."

"Any idea where they went, Gordie? "

"Don't know and don't give a damn anymore. Liz hated it here, always yearned for the bright lights, big city. Who knows? Doubt they went to Sudbury 'cause Cammy was running from Jessie. Liz told me Jessie lived somewhere near Sudbury. He was some rich old guy with more money than brains. Never met him and don't want to meet him. I'm thinking they probably headed for the big smoke in Toronto. That would be a good place to get lost in. But what do I know? I don't know nuthin."

"Thanks for your cooperation, man," Peter stated. "You've got my card. If you hear anything from your sister give me a call."

"Yeah, yeah, like she's going to call after all these years." Turning his back on Peter he followed his beer belly into the back room.

Back into his car once again Peter drove back out to Highway 17 turning south on Highway 69. He stopped for lunch in Parry Sound where he found a car wash to clean up the Mercedes and make it ready for its homecoming. He was on his way to Toronto, the home office of Moon Life Insurance. He was on his way home to his wife, Louise and, he hoped, on his way to finding Cammirand Gauthier,

Back in his Toronto office Peter slowly sipped his morning coffee and wondered where to begin his search for Cammirand. Picking up the Toronto Star his eyes glued themselves to the headlines, "Woman found dead in uptown apartment." The photo of the young woman unmistakably marked the end of his quest. "Unbelievable!" he shouted to no one there.

"Unbelievable!" Finding Cammirand Gauthier dead was a total shock. This was the last turn of events he expected. Although he had never personally met the girl he had learned to feel compassion for her. "Unbelievable!" he whispered to the uncaring empty room.

He wasted no time in getting to the police station. Over his long career in the insurance investigative field he had made some good friends there. He had helped them out with information on more than one occasion and they had done the same for him. His head was jammed with questions. He hoped to get some answers.

Talking to Officer Kennedy Peter learned that Cammirand Gauthier had been found dead in her bed. She had been working as a transcriber for a legal firm in Toronto. Her business was home-based so she wasn't expected to report to work at any particular hour but the transcripts she dutifully prepared on her computer did have due dates. When the due date of an important transcript came and went her employer placed a call to Cammirand's Toronto home. Getting no answer to his call he sent his secretary to find out what was going on. When the secretary received no answer to her knock, the superintendent was requested to open the door.

"The secretary fainted when the body was discovered," Officer Kennedy said. "The super called the police. He reported the smell was pretty bad. Guess the body had been there for a while. The coroner determined the cause of death was rat poisoning."

"Any suspects?" Peter enquired hopefully.

Officer Kennedy answered, "Sorry, Peter, I'm not at liberty to tell you that but check in with us in a day or two. I may be able to tell you more then."

Peter left the police station. He was puzzled. Had Jessie been alive he would have been the prime suspect in this case. But Jessie was dead. "Who? And why?" he wondered.

Answering those big questions was an easy task for the police, Peter later learned. His officer friend told him that in the drawer of her bedside table a diary was found. It covered events over a five year period. Cammy had detailed the terrifying victimization she endured at the brutal hands of her husband, Jessie Gauthier. She had clearly written about the kindness of Gus and Bonny Arnone, her reluctant decision to leave the safety of Bonny's grandmotherly, watchful eye to search out her friend Elizabeth Karlin in Spanish. The beating and rape that took place in the Spanish campground was described. Cammy had written that she thought one of the rapists had said something like, "This is for Elizabeth." In her journal she wrote, "I must have heard him wrong. His offhand comment made no sense to me whatsoever because Liz has been and is my one true friend in this entire messed up world."

Peter put in a call to the Arnones in Elliot Lake to inform them of the place and date of Cammirand's funeral. He knew of no one else to notify. He attended the funeral himself and shook hands with a handful of people from the legal firm where Cammy had worked.

A few weeks after the funeral he received the hoped for promotion at Moon Life Insurance for his investigative prowess. He felt totally undeserving. Sitting at his kitchen table talking to his wife, Louise, he shared all that he had learned about the now closed case of Cammirand Gauthier. "It seems that when they were in school together in Sudbury Elizabeth had a crush on this guy Jessie Gauthier," he explained. "When Cammirand married Jessie, Elizabeth was as jealous as a Jezebel but disguised her wrath in a show of phony friendship. Apparently when Cammy was on the run from Jessie and sought out Elizabeth for assistance Liz had long been plotting her revenge. She hired the guys to rape Cammy then calmly used Cammirand's blind faith in her to plan her own escape from the dreary life she shared with her brother Gordie in the Spanish campground.

Elizabeth candidly confessed to police that she felt her need for revenge had been satisfied by the brutal beating and rape." Reaching for his wife's hand Peter sought its assurance and comfort. "That should have been the end of the misery, Louise. But it wasn't."

Feeling his sadness Louise softly spoke, "Tell me all of it, Peter. Get it all out. You will feel better if you do."

Squeezing his wife's hand Peter continued, "Well, it seems that more recently both Liz and Cammy held an attraction for Brian Bartholomew, a prominent Toronto lawyer. Cammy met Brian when she was making a delivery of a transcript to her employer's office. He invited her out for lunch. Cammy accepted. Later she introduced Brian to Elizabeth who was jealous. She thought Brian was a good catch and wanted him for herself. But Brian had eyes only for Cammirand. I haven't seen it but the police told me it was all in Cammy's diary. She had written the words, "Confided in Liz my love for Brian." It seems that outwardly Liz displayed happiness for Cammy in her new relationship. But revenge is sweet and Liz was not to be outdone twice. Cammirand would not steal love from Elizabeth a second time."

Taking a deep breath Peter continued, "Elizabeth could cook and she knew of Cammy's love for Italian spaghetti and meatballs."

"No," Louise gasped. "Don't tell me."

"Yeah," Peter said. "It was the meatballs. Cammirand accepted Liz's deadly dinner invitation. After dinner she came home to die. Case closed."

"That poor girl!" Louise Lowenza whispered wiping the tears from her eyes. "Abandoned by her parents at an early age, abused and deceived by her husband, betrayed and murdered by her best friend." She sighed before asking Peter, "What will happen to the millions she was to inherit?"

Scratching his head in frustration Peter answered, "Cammy's pain, government's gain. I don't know why I should but somehow I feel responsible. If only I had worked faster, found her sooner."

"Don't beat yourself up, Peter," Louise demanded. "Don't do it. You did your best. None of this is your fault."

"And me," Peter cried, "I get the damn promotion I've been wanting for so long. Maybe it's time to think about retiring, Louise."

"You're far too young to be thinking about retirement, my love." Wanting to put the matter to bed Louise put her arm around her husband to console him. But still puzzled she couldn't really let it go. There was one thing bothering her. She had to ask. "But who was it that took the picture of Cammy when she was hiding at Bonny Vu in Elliot Lake?"

"Yeah, well, that's the part that really gets me, Louise. That photographer sent Cammy into the murderous hands of Elizabeth but it was totally unintentional. Seems he was just some guy who likes to take pictures of motel signs."

FIND FIRINN

Uncle Farlan is a lowlander in the Scottish County of Berwickshire. He is no happier about the upcoming journey than I am. "Forba, it's an unhappy day," he says to me. "Your parents have chosen to emigrate from Scotland and sadly you and I have no choice but to follow in their footsteps. We are Scots and we belong in Scotland. Aye, child, we may border with England but what is the truth of the matter? What are we, lass?"

"We are Scots, Uncle Farlan."

"Aye, and no matter where in the world we are forced to live, what are we, lass?"

"We are Scots, Uncle Farlan."

"Aye, 'tis firinn, Forba."

"What is firinn, Uncle Farlan?"

"What is firinn? The child asks what is firinn."

"I do."

"Firinn means truth, child. Let it be a lesson to you now that no matter where in the world you live you must always seek and find firinn. Do you promise, lass?"

"I do, Uncle Farlan."

"Good girl, Forba. Let it be our secret word from this day onward."

"Yes, our secret word!"

"And what is it, lass?"

"Firinn. The secret word is firinn."

"And what does it mean?"

"It means truth."

"Aye, and give me your word you'll not be forgetting it?"

"Aye, Uncle Farlan. I swear I'll not forget."

Just then my mother's shout slapped my seven-year-old ears. "Forba, come into the house. We'll be leaving soon."

"I have to go in now, Uncle Farlan. Soon we are leaving. Have you done your packing? Are you ready to go?"

"Aye, lass, my suitcase is packed but my heart has drained empty."

"Mother says we will be much better off in Canada, Uncle Farlan. She says father has a good job offered to him in Toronto. Mom says we will love the boat trip and she calls our journey a big adventure."

"Aye, my sister always did have a way of putting a fresh coat of paint on an old table."

"Forba, come into the house. I'll not be calling you again, lass. Do you want your father and me to go off to Canada without you?"

I looked into Uncle Farlan's deep blue eyes. "It's time," I say.

And now forty-nine years later I sit here, an overweight, aging woman, feeling useless as a screen door on a submarine. I feel frozen on this hard wooden chair. Uncle Farlan lies in the bed, an old man. I've been sitting here at his side every day for two months; ever since he was transferred from the hospital to Kipling Acres, the long term care facility.

He is diagnosed with prostate cancer. He did undergo surgery but the doctor tells me that my uncle's days are numbered.

My parents are gone. My mother, Susan, died seven years ago. Her passage was a painful one. Cancer filled her body and destroyed her mind. My father, Neil MacPherson, was more fortunate. He passed in his sleep three years ago; a heart attack the doctor said.

I did marry but my only marriage ended in divorce. I was never blessed with children. Uncle Farlan is the only family I have left and he doesn't know who I am.

Prostate cancer is what landed him in the hospital but Alzheimer is its partner. Between the two, somewhere in this hospital bed, the Uncle Farlan I know and love is hiding.

"Uncle Farlan, do you remember our voyage on the 'Empress of Scotland'?"

I receive no response from this old man. He offers nothing more than a blank stare.

Memory transforms him into the young man jostling his way ahead of me toward the ship. We had travelled from Berwickshire to Liverpool and now it is time to board the ship. "Keep your balance, lass," he says to me as he leads the way through the crowd. Mom and Dad are right behind me. I'm very excited.

"What a beautiful ship, Uncle Farlan. Mom is right! This will be a great adventure!"

"Aye, lass, but what is important is that you keep your balance in this crowd. Remember, my name means *son of the furrows*. And do you know what a furrow is?"

"I think I do."

"Well, in case you don't let me tell you. A furrow is a long narrow trench made in the ground."

"I know that."

"Okay, so you know that. Now the trick to keeping your balance is to make believe you are walking in this trench. "

And that is exactly what I do. I follow Uncle Farlan through the furrow until at last we arrive at the ramp ready to board the ship.

"Do you remember the day we boarded the ship in Liverpool, Uncle Farlan? Do you remember lifting me high up into your arms and setting me down again upon the ramp?"

He does not but I do remember. "Hold my hand, lass," he orders. "Stay close to me and we will be fine."

"Don't get too far ahead of us, Farlan," mother shouts.

"Always a worrier, my sister," Uncle Farlan says to me. To my mother he yells, "No worries, Susan."

I remember him bending down and with a grand smile on his face he says, "We're going to Canada, Forba."

"I know that, Uncle Farlan," I laugh.

"They have bears in Canada. Did you know that too then since you seem to know so much?"

"Are the bears friendly?" I ask.

"As friendly as the bear in Berwick," he sings aloud.

"Bears in Berwick?" By now we are in the ship and heading for our tourist class cabin.

"You're nearly there," mother shouts.

"There are no bears in Berwickshire, Uncle Farlan."

"I see, little one who knows all there is to know! And what about the bear that is chained to a wych-elm tree, lass?"

"Bear chained to a tree?"

"Aye, are you forgetting the coat of arms for the Borough of Berwick on Tweed? Don't be forgetting your homeland so fast, child."

"Oh, Uncle Farlan, I thought you meant a real bear."

*Uncle Farlan, do you remember telling me
about the bear chained to the wych-elm tree that
formed part of the insignia of Berwickshire District?*

Again he does not respond. I allow my thoughts
to cherish the memory. Our crossing of the pond is a
treat of a holiday. With Mom, Dad and Uncle Farlan I
arrive in Canada. The first stop is in the City of Quebec
where many people leave the ship. We stay on though
until the Empress of Scotland arrives in Montreal.

We stay in Montreal only long enough to get to
the bus station where we board a Greyhound Bus bound
for Toronto.

*Uncle Farlan, do you remember the day we first
arrived in Toronto?*

My parents rent a small house in the west end of
the city. Dad starts his new job and Mom settles in to
making the house our home. My childhood years are a

happy memory. Uncle Farlan plays a major role in providing that happiness.   Until I am able to find new friends in my new country Uncle Farlan is my willing playmate.

We played tag, Uncle Farlan. Surely you remember that? And hopscotch! Remember when we played hide and go seek! You must remember. And the Saturday afternoon matinees? Uncle Farlan, for years you took me with you to the movies at the Grant Theatre. Now that is something that you cannot have forgotten.

Finally Uncle Farlan agrees to speak to me. I am thrilled when he begins to talk. My exhilaration dies a quick death when I hear his first words. "Who are you?" he asks.

It's me, Uncle Farlan. It's me, Forba, your niece.

He doesn't know me. I try not to cry but the silent tears flow unbidden. Yes, of course too many years have gone by. Uncle Farlan was best man at my wedding. It was his shoulder I leaned on when my marriage ended in divorce. It was Uncle Farlan who held me in his arms and comforted me when first my mother and then my father died.

The doctor has explained to me that Alzheimer is a thief. Showing no mercy it has slipped into my uncle's mind and stolen his memories. Now I am fifty-six years old and I realize that most of my own life is behind me. I hope I still have some good years ahead but at fifty-six I cannot lie to myself and pretend I am middle-aged. How many people live to be one hundred and twelve years old? As for me I don't want to. I have no desire to out-live myself.

But one thing I have learned is that at fifty-six possibly the greatest blessing I have received in life is the ability to remember all that has gone before this very day. Alzheimer has stolen this ability from my dear uncle.

Always throughout my life I have been the observer of myself and of others. I have never been satisfied to simply know what people do. Always I have wanted to understand why people do what they do. Always I am searching and this very important part of me is there thanks only to Uncle Farlan. He is the one who taught me that I should never accept things at face value. Always I should search for the truth.

Even as a little girl it was he who had said to me, "Let it be a lesson to you now that no matter where in the world you live you must always seek and find firinn. Do you promise, lass?" And without hesitation I gave him my word.

The doctor has told me that he does not know if Uncle Farlan will ever remember me. What he said to me is, "Short term memory is gone, Forba. Your greatest hope of connecting with your uncle before he dies is to focus on events that happened long ago."

And this is what I have been doing for so very long but without any success. It breaks my heart to think that my dear Uncle Farlan will die not knowing me and not knowing how very much I love him.

I've been trying every day for a long time and I am becoming discouraged. Still I cannot give up. For as long as he has breath I must keep trying.

Again I remember him telling me, "Let it be a lesson to you now that no matter where in the world you live you must always seek and find firinn.

Uncle Farlan, do you remember that long ago day in Berwickshire when you told me about firinn?

"Firinn," he says. No, I am not imagining things or allowing my hopes to create illusion. His eyes appear brighter. I see a long-remembered twinkle. He does speak and he repeats the word, "Firinn."

Uncle Farlan, that is our secret word. Do you remember? Do you remember that firinn is our secret word?

"Aye, and give me your word you'll not be forgetting it." His voice is weak but his words are clear.

"I did give you my word, Uncle Farlan. And I have never forgotten. All my life I have followed your advice. I have always tried to search for truth. My goal has always been to find firinn."

"Is that you sitting there on that chair, Forba?"

The floodgates open. At last he remembers my name. He knows who I am. "Aye, it's me, Uncle Farlan."

"You're not a little girl anymore, Forba."

"Indeed I am not, Uncle."

"But you remember our secret word."

"Finding firinn is an integral part of what I am," I answer.

"And what are you, child?" he questions with eyes that shine and I know he is right there with me. "What are we?"

I am thoughtful but only for a moment while I wait for the long ago memory to reach my lips. Yes, I had forgotten but now I know just what to say. "We are Scots, Uncle Farlan."

"Aye, and no matter where in the world we are forced to live, what are we, lass?"

"We are Scots, Uncle Farlan."

"Aye, 'tis firinn, Forba," he whispers.

"Aye, Uncle Farlan. I'll not forget."

I hold his hand in mine. I lean over and kiss his tired brow.

I will forever appreciate that my dear uncle knew me in his last hour. I am grateful that he did not die alone. Always I will remain thankful that I was at his side until the very last moment of his life.

AFTER WORDS

With trepidation John snapped shut his laptop. He sat on his chair and stared downward at his quivering liver-spotted hands. Before today he merely ignored the age spots and wrinkles but that was before he had typed the word, yes, into his last message.

An English teacher for more than thirty years John Rowe, now retired, had always impressed on the vulnerable young minds of his students the fact that words most definitely are important. No one knew better than him that once a word is spoken there is no taking it back. He could not deny that in his messaging with Mary he had perhaps exaggerated.

Throughout the six months he had been sharing on-line messages with Mary he had easily convinced himself that he was, indeed, a young sixty-two. Sitting alone in his library tap, tapping the words onto the screen he had found it quite an easy matter and sometimes a downright amusing one to create an attractive, adventurous character whose attributes were far removed from those he possessed.

Moving away from his desk John left the library and walked down the hallway to his bedroom. He stood before the mirror which hung on the wall behind his dresser. His weak blue eyes noted the sparse white hairs atop a face whose skin was sagging downward toward total collapse upon his goitered neck. He considered a wig. Did he have time to buy one? Or perhaps he could run out to the shop and buy some hair dye. He wished he had not told Mary he had black hair.

And why did he fabricate the story about the Caribbean cruise and tell her he was deeply tanned? He wondered if this was something else he could buy in a bottle to disguise the purple veins that ran atop his nose and the deep etches on his forehead. When did the wrinkles become etchings? He couldn't remember.

John did remember his grandsons who, with childhood audacity, boldly stated, "You sure have a lot of wrinkles, Granddad!"

"And I earned every one of them, lads!" John replied. "If you work hard and deal with life's trials you will earn some wrinkles too."

Perhaps the wrinkles became etchings when Margaret died. His beautiful Margaret with the flowing brown tresses was murdered by cancer in the prime of her life; too soon to become acquainted with the young boys who called him Granddad or sometimes Gramps when in a more playful mood.

John forced his mind to return to the present. Mary would not be overjoyed to meet a balding Gramps for dinner that evening.

Thinking about dinner caused his stomach to rumble. He was hungry. He left his bedroom and walked further down the hallway to the kitchen at the back of his old house.

Margaret had been a fine cook. Since her death he had learned how to keep himself alive by opening cans and nuking frozen dinners. Occasionally his daughter poked her head into his life and stocked his freezer with remnants of the meals she prepared for his grandsons. Once in a while she would stock the refrigerator with fresh fruits and vegetables but she soon got tired of tossing her purchases into the garbage can when she later discovered them rotted in the crisper. She ceased buying fresh vegetables in favour of the frozen variety that John simply needed to heat up atop the stove in a pot filled with a little water.

Since Margaret's passing John spent his long days in a methodical fashion. He was 50 years of age when she died. He was too young to retire and decided to continue teaching for another ten years. At the age of sixty he checked his bank balance and being mortgage-free he made the sensible decision to stop working.

Since retirement John would breakfast at eight a.m. It was always Cheerios with a spot of milk, a glass of orange juice and a slice of toast with raspberry jam.

After breakfast he would go for a walk-about through the small town's residential streets until he came to the park where he would sit on the bench and stare out at the lake. Even on rainy days or blustery winter days John would keep to his routine. If necessary he would carry his big, black umbrella or don a toque to keep the cold from penetrating through his thin white hair to his pink scalp.

By ten a.m. he would be home again. Before he impulsively bought the laptop he would spend his morning puttering about the house; dusting a table or watering a plant. His laundry would mysteriously disappear from the clothes hamper and re-appear neatly folded in his dresser drawers or hanging in his bedroom closet while he occupied the park bench. Yes, Margaret had done a fine job raising their daughter. She had kept her own key to the family home long after she had moved into her own home with her husband who helped to raise his lively grandsons.

By noon John would be hungry and ready to eat his lunch.

His afternoons would be spent lounging in his easy chair with a good book until three p.m. when he would switch on the television to catch the BBC News which he was convinced was the only reliable news broadcasting station. At precisely four p.m. he would leave the house and walk into the commercial part of town where he would rent a movie; usually an action film or a science fiction drama into which he would escape each evening after supper. Once the movie finished John would take his daily shower after which he would climb into his pyjamas and go to his bed. He always kept a book on his bedside table and he would often, though not always, read until he fell sleep.

Everything changed six months ago when John bought a laptop. He'd been on his way, as usual, to the movie rental store to rent his daily video. A new computer store had opened up in town. It was situated right next door to the video store. John impulsively wandered into the new store and surprised himself when he put the purchase of the laptop on his credit card. One thing seemed to lead to another. He needed to hire a fellow to come in and hook everything up. He needed to hire an internet server. He needed to learn a whole new language, not an easy thing to do when you are seventy-eight years of age, but achieve it he did.

Words such as e-mail, surfing the net and googling became an integral part of his vocabulary. But what brought about the dramatic awareness of wrinkles, brown-spotted hands and purple-veined nose was John's discovery of the Senior Chat room.

The laptop turned his life upside down. No longer did he dust the tables, rent the movies or pay attention to the BBC News.

Instead he chatted.

And he had been chatting with Mary for nearly six months. He became very creative in expressing himself in the chat room. He drew a picture of a man that he had only read about or watched perform in his daily movies. He introduced Mary to an affable, well-travelled, middle-aged man; well, maybe not middle-aged at sixty-two, but certainly not the old gramps his daughter checked in on every day to be certain he was eating and staying alive.

The chatting was fun. It was something John relished and enjoyed but now she had invited him to meet in the real world. That was all well and good. But, even though he knew he had done so, John found it impossible to believe he had said yes. He had agreed to meet Mary that evening at five p.m.

Now in his kitchen he put together a ham and cheese sandwich. He knew he had no choice but to disappoint Mary. If he didn't meet her she would be hurt. If he met her she would be even more disappointed to meet the old man he truly was.

Mary had described herself as a recent retiree in her mid fifties; a pretty, slim woman with dark hair and brown eyes. She was young enough to be his daughter. John felt like a fool.

He decided to visit the restaurant at the appointed time for no other reason than to see her loveliness. Later he could type into his laptop an appropriate excuse for standing her up.

At five p.m. John stamped the snow off his boots and entered the tea-room. He recognized her sitting alone at a table near the back of the room. Mary looked exactly as she had described herself.

John knew he should leave but he couldn't resist the opportunity to gaze at her beauty. He decided to sit down and have a cup of tea.

Assured of a clear view he slid onto a seat across from an ordinary plump, grey-haired woman who sat alone sipping her tea. As he did so the old lady

looked up, smiled warmly and greeted him, "Hello,

John. At last we meet!"

JOSHUA'S JOURNEY

I woke up this morning with a bad taste in my mouth. Why they have to wake me up so darn early I got no idea. Why can't they let a man sleep in once in a while? It's not like I'm going anywhere. At least that's what I let them think but I'm going all right! No question about that. I'm going. Not staying here in this damn place any longer than I have to!

"Good morning, Joshua!" the fat nurse chortles.

I want to take that bad taste out of my mouth and spit it into her eye. . "Yeah, and what's good about it?"

My knees hurt. Somehow I manage to drag my legs off the bed and land my feet onto the floor. Gotta pee.

"Happy birthday, Joshua!"

"You still here?" I wish she would get outa my room. I forgot today's my birthday. Nothing happy about that. Even before I was born I had more marks against me than the dirty rug on the front hall stairs. That was a long time ago and I don't remember everything but what I can't remember my mama told me about. My mama was none too happy about that birth day. She told me I was born on July 13th, 1927.

"Everybody knows thirteen is an unlucky number. And if that isn't bad enough you were born on a Wednesday. Everybody knows Wednesday's child is full of woe." Mama said.

And if that wasn't bad enough I was born black to a white mama. The world called me a bastard. They called my mama a slut.

Gotta get me into that bathroom. "Hand me that walker so I can get myself into that bathroom! Why'd you move it way over there anyway? I always keep it right here beside my bed."

"Sorry, Joshua."

"Sorry don't do me no good. Keep that walker right here beside my bed where it belongs!"

I feel a little better now I've been to the toilet. Gotta get myself dressed and make my way over to the dining room. I'm hungry. Don't want to miss breakfast. I pull a white shirt outa the dresser drawer. Arthritis has done a number on my fingers and it's a tricky business doing up the buttons.

"Do you want any help with that shirt, Joshua?"

"Lordy, lady! You still here? Don't need no help!"

"Okay, you have a good day! I'm leaving now"

"Good! It's about time!" I get the buttons all done up. I pull the grey pants outa the closet and carry them back to the bed where I plunk myself down. Never used to have this trouble getting into my pants. Used to stand up tall, slide in one leg, then the other; tighten the belt and away I'd go. I remember those days. Some people call them the good old days. Not me!

Getting into my pants is a project and I don't mean the kind I used to live in either. Anyway by the time I was three mama moved out of that hell-hole and rented a little house near Oakwood and Vaughan. Don't know where my daddy was but he sure wasn't in that neighbourhood. Back in those days I was the only black face in the crowd. I asked mama once where my daddy was but she wasn't in a good mood to give me a straight answer.

Mama used to say if her life was a movie it would be a melodrama. If my life was a movie it would probably be a comedy or maybe a horror show depending on how you want to look at it.

I get my pants on. The pants legs are dragging on the floor; way too long. I shove my big, old feet into my shoes and it makes no difference. The pants legs are still dragging. The pants are old and I know they're not getting any longer. Means I'm getting shorter. I didn't notice the shrinking. Guess it was a gradual thing. Doesn't seem long ago that I was six feet tall. Of course I wasn't bow-legged in those days. Don't know when that happened either.

Today's my birthday. Not sure but I think I'm 82 years old. Doesn't seem long since I was a strapping young man. In fact it doesn't seem that long ago that I was a kid. This gray fuzz on my head was curly black in those days. I was the only black kid in my school.

106

When I was little I didn't know the difference between black and white but by the time I was ten I knew how to punch out anybody that got in my way or called me a bad name. I was brutal when I had to be. I knew how to be tough and even cruel. It kept people away from me and that's how I liked it.

I remember the day I was sitting out on the front step. Mama was at work and I was just hanging around, bored, waiting for her to come home to make us some supper. I saw this old lady coming down the sidewalk pulling her grocery cart. From the step I could see she had some good stuff in that cart. There was bread, apples, some meats from the butcher shop wrapped up in brown paper and tied with strings. I wanted some of that good stuff. I was hungry.

When that old lady was just about in front of me I stuck my leg out in front of her. The cart collapsed, groceries scattered all over the cement and she went flying. Then down she went on the sidewalk. Her knees were bleeding all over the place. It was hilarious. Stupid old woman!

Before she had a chance to pick herself up I grabbed a package of meat and ran up the alleyway like I was being chased by dragons. Once I was safely hidden in the back alley I opened the brown package. Good stuff! To this day knackwurst is one of my favourite sausages but it has never tasted as good as it did that day.

Mama came home about a half hour later. I remember she cooked a good big supper. I wasn't hungry but I could always eat. Then because it was Wednesday night mama hauled me off to a mid-week prayer meeting at the Baptist Church.

That's a long time ago. I don't go to church these days. I don't go anywhere. Last time I went to church they caught me stealing the candle. Never set foot inside a church again after that.

I hate these pants flopping down on the floor when I walk. Even with the walker I think I'm gonna get tripped up so I head on back to my bed to sit down. Bending over, I roll up my pants legs. That's better. I'm gonna head down to that dining room now to get some breakfast.

I'm walking down the hall minding my own business and this old guy steps up beside me. "You goin' down for breakfast?" he asks.

"None of your business where I'm going! Leave me alone!"

That old man brings back some memories. I remember walking down that school hallway minding my own business. Out of nowhere these four white guys are blocking my path. I showed them a thing or two. It wasn't for nothing I carried that knife in my pocket. I managed to cut three of them. The fourth one I knocked down and kicked the shit out of him. The odds were against me but I did good.

Of course the principal didn't admire my tactics. I was suspended. I didn't care. I decided to quit. I never liked school anyway.

Mama wasn't happy about me quitting school. I don't like remembering her tears. I knew she had enough to worry about getting herself from one day into the next without having to bother about me. Anyway by this time I didn't much care what mama thought. It was time for me to strike out on my own.

I guess you might say I was lucky getting a job right away the way that I did. I was talking with the fellow who owned the corner store in our neighbourhood and while I was doing that another

fellow came in carrying a bunch of newspapers.   I
stood back and listened to him talking to the owner.
"This will be my last delivery," he said. "I've got a
better job at the tool and die factory; starting Monday."

"Hey Mister," I asked, "what do I have to do to
get your job delivering these newspapers?"

Well, the fellow gave me the address of The
Toronto Star. I didn't waste any time getting
downtown.   The man who interviewed me said I
reminded him of Mr. Atkinson.

"Who's Mr. Atkinson?" I asked.

I was told that he was a printer who took over
the running of The Toronto Star. "As a boy he knew
only hardship and need. After his mama died Joe
Atkinson left school to go to work at the age of 14.
Somehow you remind me of Mr. Atkinson. I'm gonna
take a chance and hire you, Joshua.

I started working for the Toronto Star in 1941. I stayed with them for nearly 50 years; been delivering papers all my life. When I got my first pay cheque I moved out of mama's house into my own room in a downtown rooming-house. I got a real deal on my room. Told the landlady I was an orphan. Just like I figured, she felt sorry for me and gave me a discount on the rent. Dumb bitch! She believed everything I told her. I told the same story to the guy who ran the neighbourhood restaurant. I got free meals anytime I wanted them. He was as stupid as my landlady! Suckers all of them!

They are all suckers here at the home too! Hate this place but the food smells good. I take my place at a table where there's no one else sitting. I like to be left alone. A pretty young lady sets a plateful of good breakfast food in front of me. I see two eggs sunny-side up; four strips of bacon, crispy just the way I like it, and two thick slices of buttered toast. I notice the young lady is pretty. I notice this because I haven't had a lot of pretty ladies in my life.

I remember one woman though. I met her at one of the stores when I was delivering my papers. I was nearly thirty years old by that time. Her name was Sharon and she was black like me. She had beautiful, big brown eyes and a smile that could light up a city on a stormy night. I got up some whiskey courage one night and asked her to come out for a drive. I wasn't much good with women so I was surprised when she accepted my invitation.

I picked her up outside the store the next night in my truck. I got a good deal on my truck the year before. I was really smart that time. I hobbled onto the car lot pretending I had an injured leg. The salesman asked, "Hey, what happened to your leg?"

I had to think fast on my feet. "I was badly burned pulling a little girl out of a burning house couple years back. Lost the good use of this leg." I answered. "Really hoping I can get a good deal on a truck so I can give this leg a rest. It's tough on a guy walking all over town."

Well, the fellow must have been a few cards short of a full deck. He was dumb enough to believe every word I told him. He gave me an unbelievable good price for the pick-up. I made my buy and once behind the wheel I felt great. I conned him good and the guy was too stupid to know it. Even thinking about it today makes me want to laugh.

So I picked Sharon up the next night in my truck. She looked pretty in her blue skirt. I could see a little bit of her lacy crinoline underneath. She was wearing a stripy kind of pink blouse with a polka-dotted neckerchief around her neck. I pointed my Chevy truck

114

north and we drove up Yonge Street until we were out of the city limits. "You like driving in the country?" I asked her.

"It's beautiful," she said. "I never get a chance to escape big city life. This is nice."

"So how long you been working in that store, Sharon?"

"Oh, I don't work there," she said. "I was just in there buying some gum when you came in delivering those newspapers."

"So, where do you work then?"

You could have knocked me over with a feather when I heard her answer, "I don't go to work. I go to school."

I burned some rubber when I hit that brake. I turned off the ignition and turned in my seat to face her.

She looked soft and angelic sitting there with those big, brown, trusting eyes. Innocent wasn't a big word in my vocabulary but that's what she was; a school girl. And there I was nearly thirty years old out in my pick-up with a damn kid.

"How old are you, Sharon?" I asked.

"Nearly fifteen," she giggled.

"Oh, my God! Out!" I shouted. "Get outa my truck. I got no plan to go to jail because of some stupid kid out for a joy ride in my truck. Out!"

I'll never forget the look on her face when I left her standing there on the side of that country road. I didn't care how long it took her to walk back to the city. No skin off my nose! Dumb-ass kid!"

The next morning I went to work as usual. I picked up the papers, threw them into the back of my truck to start my daily deliveries. It wasn't until I got to the variety store where I'd met Sharon that I actually took a look at the papers. And there it was in mammoth letters. "SCHOOL GIRL FOUND RAPED AND MURDERED ON DESERTED COUNTRY ROAD."

I have to admit I was shocked to see Sharon's picture there in that paper. Dumb kid! She had plenty of time to walk back to the city before nightfall. Bet she was too lazy to walk and stupid enough to accept a ride from some stranger. Thank goodness nobody knew she'd been in my truck. Boy, I sure learned a big lesson that day. Never had no woman in my truck ever again unless she showed me proof that she was over twenty-one. Sharon sure fooled me. Fool me once, shame on you! I don't know if they ever caught the guy that killed her. Can't remember ever seeing it in the paper so guess he got away with it.

So I notice the young pretty lady who served me my breakfast. I don't know why she reminds me of Sharon because Sharon was black and this girl isn't white or black. I don't know what she is so I decided to ask her. "Where are you from?"

"I'm from the Philippines," she says.

"Where's that?" I ask again.

"Far away," she answers and then she was gone.

I finish my breakfast, take a tight hold on my walker, and head back to my room. I don't want to go back to my room. I hate being locked up in here with all these old codgers. I want to go back to my old room in Toronto. I'm not going to stay in this damn place any longer than I have to. I need a plan.

I get back to my room, sit down in my lazy-boy chair and decide to take a nap until lunch time.

There's not a lot in this world I care about but I'm a man who likes a good meal. I go back again to the dining room when lunch time rolls around. I look at all the tables. There are people sitting at every one of them. I don't know what to do. I'm thinking I'll head back to my room. I hate sharing a table with these people. They always want to talk. I'm not looking for any friends. I don't want a friend. I had a friend once and a fat lot of good that did me.

Eddy was my friend. Ha! Why am I thinking about Eddy? I must be getting old remembering all this crap from the early days. I was close to forty when I met Eddy. I was a loner and I like being a loner but this particular afternoon I was just finishing work for the day. I was climbing the stairs on the way to my room. My plan was to get cleaned up and head on out to the local diner for a good hot supper after a hard day's work. So I'm climbing up the stairs and this guy is coming down the stairs. He's carrying a big box full of old clothes. The box is bigger than he is and he can hardly see where he's going. So, of course, he walks right into me and nearly knocks me down. Shirts, pants, underwear, socks; clothes all over the stairwell.

The idiot stands there looking at me like it's my fault. "Can you help me pick this stuff up?" he asks.

"Why the hell should I help you? I should knock your block off. You nearly sent me flying down these stairs!"

So there he is, helter-skelter, going here, going there and picking up these crappy old clothes. "Sorry," he mutters. "I didn't see you coming."

"Yeah, well, watch where you're going next time!" I told him and carried on up to my room.

Damned if he didn't turn around and follow me. I reached my door and there he was breathing onions over my shoulder. "Hey, what do you think you're doing?" I asked. "Get away from my door!"

Instead of leaving he stands his ground. "Mister, can you help me out? I got kicked out of my room. I got no money; no place to go. All I got in this world is this box of old clothes."

"What do I look like, the Salvation Army?" I shouted. "What do I care what you got or where you go?"

But the dumb nut wouldn't move out of my way. I barely had room enough to move my arm to get the key out of my pocket and into its lock.

"Please, mister. I lost my job. I'm desperate."

"What's in it for me?" I want to know.

"You can have these clothes, mister."

"What do I want with a bunch of your old clothes?"

"You're about my size. You can wear them, mister."

"When's the last time you had a meal?" I asked.

"Can't remember," he says.

Okay, so call me a fool! I let him stow his stuff in my room for a few weeks until he finds a job. He sleeps on the couch and after a little while I get used to having him around. When he starts working and gets a room of his own once again we still get together three or four times a week. We meet at the diner and have supper together. He's the only friend I ever had. Some friend! Out of the blue one night he tells me he's met a girl. He's going to get married, move to Alberta and take a job in a store the girl's father owns.

Just like that he's going to leave town. I don't need to jump in a lake to know the water's wet. I wasn't born yesterday. Some friend! I decided I'd fix his wagon. I got the name and address of his girlfriend's father, sent him a letter telling him all about Eddy's prison record and how he was planning to take off for Alberta leaving his wife and kids high and dry here in Toronto.

Two weeks later Eddy's back, banging on my door. "Joshua," he says, "I don't know why but she dropped me like a hot potato! Can I stay with you a couple days till I find myself another room?"

Oh, so Eddy didn't like being dropped? Well, I'd show him. "My heart bleeds for you, Eddy. Get lost!"

Yeah, I had a friend once and I don't want another one.

So I'm looking around the dining room. There's not a single unoccupied table. Hunger decides not to let me return to my room. So, like an idiot, I stand there with my tongue hanging out and my nose smelling what I'm pretty sure is roast beef with gravy.

Then out of the blue the pretty Philippino lady, plates in hand, is on her way to one of the tables.

"Hi, Joshua. Take a seat," she says on her way past me.

I'm still standing there when she makes her way back to the kitchen. "Joshua, why don't you sit down and I'll bring your lunch to you?"

"I don't want to sit with nobody. I like being left alone," I say.

The dumb woman smiles at me and says, "I've got an idea. You can sit with Victoria."

"Who the hell is Victoria?"

"Victoria is my daughter. And I want you to watch your language when you are with her. She's having her lunch in the kitchen. You can sit with her. She'll be good company for you."

"There's nothing wrong with my language. I don't want no company. And I don't like kids."

"You like roast beef, don't you?"

I have to admit she's got a point there. I relent. "Okay, okay, so I'll sit with the kid in the kitchen."

I follow her out to the kitchen. The cook is there rattling the pots and pans. There's a young kid scraping the plates and filling the dishwasher. "It's noisy in here. I don't like it!"

"There's a lot you don't like, eh, Joshua?" she laughs.

"I don't see nothing funny about that," I snap. I start to turn my walker and head back to my room but then I see the cook slicing the roast beef onto a plate. "Okay, so where do I sit?"

I'm sitting across the table from the little girl. She's maybe nine or ten years old. I remember I was a good fighter when I was this kid's age.

"Tripped up any old ladies lately?" I ask her.

"That's a very stupid question, mister."

"Yeah, and what's so stupid about it? When I was your age I knew how to handle myself."

She sat and stared at me for a minute then she says, "What's your name, mister?"

"Who wants to know?" I answer.

"I'm Victoria and I want to know."

"Yeah, well, it's none of your business."

"I'm making plans, mister."

"What plans?" I ask.

"It's none of your business," she snaps.

Well, blow me down! I can't stop laughing. This girl has spunk. I decide I like her. She's a lot like me. I stop laughing when the pretty lady sets the plate of roast beef, potatoes and gravy in front of me. "You're laughing" she says. "I knew Victoria would be good for you!" Then she's gone.

"What's your pretty mama's name?" I ask Victoria.

"That's none of your business either, mister. Even my mother doesn't know about my plans."

"Yeah," I say, "Well, I don't care about your plans. I got a plan of my own."

"What's your plan, mister?"

"Why should I tell you my plan? You gonna tell me yours?"

"I will if you will," she says.

The kid had me curious. Besides I guess it won't kill me to talk about my plan. Maybe talking about it will help me to figure out how I'm going to achieve it. "Okay," I says, "I'm planning to blow this joint! I'm gonna get outa here and move back to my room in the city."

"You gonna run away?" she asks me.

"Yep. I'm gonna run away."

"How you gonna run away when you can hardly walk without that old walker?" she asks me. "You're not going to run anywhere, mister. But I am!"

"What do you mean, you are?"

"I'm gonna run away from home."

"And just where do you think you're going? "

"I'm going to the Philippines. I'm gonna find my daddy and live with him."

"You got a daddy in the Philippines? Where's the Philippines?"

"It's far away." she says.

"And how do you think a little kid like you is going to travel far away all by herself? Are you gonna leave your pretty mama and take off just like that?"

"I can take care of myself. Don't worry about me, mister!"

"So who's worried?" I say. "Did you ever meet your daddy, kid?"

"Nope, but I'm gonna find him!"

"I never met my daddy either. I'm an old man now and it don't matter no more. You know what, kid? I wasn't much older than you when I struck out on my own. I had no daddy. I left my mama and I spent my life alone. Being alone is how I like it."

"I'm not gonna be alone," Victoria insists. "I'm gonna be with my daddy."

"Just how far away is this place called Philippines? Maybe I'll go there with you."

"Who asked you?" she blurts. "I don't need no old man in a walker coming with me. Anyway I like being alone. I'm going by myself."

"And just when are you planning to leave?"

"Nosy parker! Nosy parker! Mind your own beeswax!"

The kid gets up from the table and walks out of the kitchen. I sit there wondering what I should do. I finish eating my roast beef, look all around the big kitchen but I can't see the pretty Philippino lady. Maybe I should find her and tell her about the kid's plan to run away from home. But then, why should I? It's no skin off my nose. I don't even like kids.

I'm getting up from the table. I reach for my walker and begin my journey back to my room. I leave the kitchen and as I walk through the dining room towards the exit I see the pretty lady coming my way. "Did you enjoy your lunch, Joshua?" she asks.

"You're a mama," I say.

"Yes, Joshua. I'm a mama. Victoria is my baby."

"I remember my mama. She was pretty too. I left her when I was a kid, not much older than your daughter."

"That must have broken her heart, Joshua. Did you ever go back to see her?"

"Nope, I never did. I figured she was better off without me hanging around her neck, holding her back. See, my mama was a white lady. In those days a white lady with a black kid had no chance of a future."

"Joshua, I wouldn't care what colour my child was. If she was purple I'd still want her with me. Don't you know true love is colour blind?"

"True love is colour blind, you say? No, I never thought of it that way. You love your little girl?"

"More than life, Joshua."

"Hmm, well, pretty lady, I like being by myself. I don't care about other people and I never did learn to like kids. But I met your Victoria. She's got spunk. She kind of reminds me of myself when I was a kid."

"Oh, she's got spunk, all right, Joshua!"

"Pretty lady, I probably should mind my own business but there's something about Victoria you've got to know."

"What is it? Tell me, Joshua."

"Pretty lady, I'm an old man and I don't know if I believe in redemption or not but maybe there's one good thing I can do before I blow this pop stand. Now, you sit down and listen closely to what I have to say. Maybe this can be my birthday present to me."

HOPE OF GLORY

I can barely hear Linda whispering. I want to tell her to speak louder but my voice refuses to do what it's told. "Whatever happens stay away from Peter!"

I guess she is afraid I can't hear her because she keeps repeating the same thing over and over again until it is getting a little monotonous. *Peter who* I want to ask. Then I find myself wracking my brain trying to remember who I know with the name of Peter. I can't think of a single person that I've ever met in my long sixty-five years of life with the name of Peter.

My sister has reached through the side rails of this stiff, sanitary, old-fangled hospital bed and she is holding my hand tight like she's scared to let go. I can't remember a time before this when Linda has voluntarily held my hand.

Sure I can remember lots of times when we were little kids and my dear mother would shout out after us, "Take your sister's hand, Lester! Keep your eye on her now!"

That was bad enough on school days but at least once we got to school I had some freedom. On Saturdays it was a different story. On Saturdays Mom worked downtown in the department store and that meant I was stuck with Linda all day. "Take your sister's hand, Lester!"

What fourteen year old boy wants to hold hands with his seven year old sister? A kid half my age she was nothing but an embarrassment to me in front of my friends. "You gotta bring her with you again? Geez, it aint natural having a little kid running the streets with us; specially a girl kid!"

You can bet your life I didn't want to take her with me to the Saturday afternoon movie at the Grant Theatre, to the baseball game at the park, to meet my friends for a cherry coke at The Dundee Restaurant or to the alley behind the house where I met with these same friends to smoke a butt or drink a cold beer stolen from the ice box of one of their unsuspecting fathers.

Linda didn't want to come with me anymore than I wanted to drag her along. "Don't want to go with Lester," she would cry to our mother. "I wanna play double-dutch with my own friends."

In those long ago days Mom was rock stubborn and determined. She would not be moved. "You will stay with your brother, Linda, and I don't want to hear another word about it! Lester, you hold your sister's hand and don't take your eyes off her. There is no rest for the wicked and I've got to go to work. There is no one else to look after her. I'm depending on you, Lester!"

I don't know if remembering those childhood days makes me want to laugh or cry. Dad died when I was ten years old. Linda was just a baby, barely three. I don't recall a lot about my Dad but one thing I do remember is the fact that he didn't leave behind a lot of financial security for Mom. "There's barely enough insurance to bury him," I overheard my Mom telling my Aunt Marcy.

It was soon after my Dad died that Mom got hired at Simpsons Department Store as a sales clerk. Mom couldn't afford to hire a baby-sitter. Our only living relative was my Aunt Marcy but she was no help because she lived with her own family way north of the city. So from the time I was ten it was my job to take care of Linda after school on week days and all day every Saturday while Mom was at work.

Sunday was my only day off but even then Mom would send us both off to Sunday School. "It's the only chance I have to get any housework done around here, Lester. There is no rest for the wicked! Now be a good boy and take her along to the Sunday School with you. And make sure you hold your sister's hand! I'm counting on you son."

We grew older and soon my Sunday School days were behind me. By the time Linda was nine I would take her by the hand but only for the time it took us to get out of Mom's view. A block from the house I'd let go of her saying, "You're on your own kid. Behave yourself and meet me here at four-thirty when Sunday School is finished. I'll take your hand and drag you home just in case Mom sees us coming."

"Okay, Lester," she would say before taking off. I never knew if she went to Sunday School or if she went to find her friends to play skipping or house or who knows what little girls at that age want to play. Whatever she did she was always there to meet me ready to go home at four-thirty. She never ratted on me. Linda was a good kid.

When Linda celebrated her tenth birthday Mom finally gave me the break I had been hoping for. At last she said to Linda, "I guess you're old enough now to look after yourself but keep an eye on this brother of yours. I'm not so sure about him."

The sad thing about Mom's statement is that she wasn't joking. At seventeen I was a little on the wild side I guess you could say. No trouble with the law but only because I was lucky. Two of my buddies were already spending time in reform school.

It's funny but all those years of holding Linda's hand had kept me out of trouble. I mean how can a guy take part in a car theft or a break-in when he's got a little kid tied to him? But by the time Linda was nine and I celebrated by drinking beer with my buddies on my sixteenth birthday I was nothing more than an accident waiting to happen.

My sister Linda graduated high school and started going to work with Mom at Simpsons Department Store. When she was twenty she married a fellow who also worked there. A few years later she was Mom to a couple of kids and along with her husband Tom she was a proud home owner. Yes, Linda was living the Canadian dream.

I was incarcerated for the first time when I was twenty-nine. I was on a break and enter job with one of my buddies. We thought there was nobody home. The guy surprised me, came up behind me and grabbed my arm. Instinct took over. I slugged the guy, knocked him down. I swear to God I didn't mean to kill him. My buddy took off. I remember him shouting at me to get going but I was frozen to the spot. I couldn't move.

At some point the guy's wife and kids came home. I

remember her screaming. Still I could not move. I

listened as her son called 911. The cops arrested me

when they arrived. Still I couldn't move. They had to

drag me out of that house.

I was charged with murder. There was a jury

trial. I was guilty and that was the verdict of the jury.

So I went to prison and there I stayed for many long

years.

I was nearly fifty years old when I was released

from jail. I had a lot of trouble finding work. Seems

nobody wants to hire an ex-con; especially one who is a

professed murderer. I met up with some of my old

buddies and before I knew it, I was making a living

pushing drugs onto poor kids who didn't know what the

hell they were getting themselves into. I didn't feel

good about myself but not bad enough to try to turn my life around.

My Mom washed her hands of me when I was in jail. Linda was the only one who came to visit me but once she had her babies she was busy and it wasn't as easy for her to get away from the house to come see her good-for-nothing brother. Soon her visits stopped.

But the day I was released from prison it was Linda who was there with her car to pick me up and take me to a room she had rented for me. She visited me a few times there but when she realized I was back in the old lifestyle she said, "I can't get involved in this crap, Lester. I wish you would get your life straightened out. Get a real job and stay out of trouble."

When I didn't take the steps to follow her advice she told me, "Sorry Lester but I can't come see you anymore. And I don't want you coming near my house. You're a bad influence on my kids. I just can't have it and besides my husband Larry will kill you if you come to the house so just stay away, okay?"

I didn't see my mother or my little sister for a lot of years after that. But the devil caught up with me. The last time I was in prison I got sick. They diagnosed me and told me I had cancer of the liver. Just last week they transferred me over to the hospital. I guess they called my sister because I know I didn't. Nobody was more surprised than me to see Linda coming into my hospital room this morning.

And here she is whispering over and over, "No matter what happens stay away from Peter."

I feel very weak but finally after much effort I am able to muster up some strength. I pour it into my voice. "Peter who?" I ask her.

"Why St. Peter, of course," she answered. She squeezed my hand harder and whispered, "I'm scared for your soul, Lester. I'm afraid he won't let you in. You will have to find a way to sneak in. Stay away from him, promise?"

Then she started to bawl her eyes out.

I hated to hear her cry. "Sorry I haven't been a good brother to you, Linda. You deserved a lot better than a waste of time like me."

"You were always good to me when I was a kid," she said.

"Only because Mom made me."

"Nah, I don't believe that Lester. You always held my hand. You kept the tough guys away from me. You were a good brother to me and you were the only Dad I knew."

"I think losing Dad is what put me on the wrong road, Linda. Everything went wrong after he died."

"Not everything, Lester. You were there for me," she said.

That's the last thing I remember. The next thing I know I arrive at the Gates of Heaven. I remember Linda's warning but there is nothing I can do. There is no way I can sneak into the place. I'm standing there and right in front me is St. Peter himself.

He is tall and regal. He has a bulbous nose, flowing white hair and a long white beard. He is authoritative in his flowing white gown. All of a sudden I am remembering all the times I refused to go to Sunday School. I remember the poor guy I murdered. It doesn't matter that I didn't mean to kill the man. I had no business breaking into his house. I had no business pushing drugs on kids. I had no business doing any of the bad things I did throughout my life.

"I hear your thoughts, Lester," he says. Then St. Peter asks the question, "Tell me what you did in life that makes you worthy of entering the gates of Heaven?"

I fall to my knees. I am ashamed. I have no defense to offer.

"Tell me!"

"There is nothing to tell, sir," I answer. "I wasted my life. I did nothing of value; nothing that can be considered worthy."

I stayed down close to the white cloud I was kneeling on while St. Peter started leafing through this huge book. He perused several pages before saying,

"I'm inclined to agree with you. I think you've arrived at the wrong gate."

Prepared to turn to meet the devil himself and to spend eternity in hell, I stood up to leave.

"No, don't go yet," Peter insisted. "It's not like our guides to make such a mistake. It is written that if you have faith, even as small as a mustard seed, you can say mountain move and it will move. Nothing will be impossible. I can't imagine what it is but there must be some reason someone thought you deserved this opportunity."

I watched as he licked his finger and kept turning the pages in the big book.

By this time I had lost even the tiniest hope of glory. But just when I thought that all was lost I heard St. Peter exclaim, "Oh, there it is! This must be your key to the golden gate!"

"My key?" I dared to ask.

"You have a sister," he replied.

"Yes, I do, sir."

"That's right. Your sister Linda."

"Yes, sir."

"Yes, this is your key. Did you know that for more than fifty years Linda has been praying for you every night before she goes to sleep? Did you know that?"

"No, sir, I didn't know."

"Hmm, seems there is a lot you didn't know but fortunately for you, your sister Linda's faith remained strong. The Master tells me we are to take you in because Linda vouches for you. She tells us you have a good heart. She tells us that you held her hand when she was a young fearful child. Is it true you held your sister's hand?"

"Yes, sir."

"Well, all right then. The Master agrees to give you a chance. Here he comes now. Reach out and take the hand of your Father. He will lead you where you need to be."

I am overcome with joy. "Thank you, sir. Thank you, God. And, Linda, I hope you can hear me. Thank you, sis."

"Look downward, my son," the Master ordered.

I look down through the white clouds and there I can see myself lying in the stiff, sanitary hospital bed. I see my sister Linda sitting on the chair, her hand reaching through the side rails.

"What do you see, my child?" God asks.

"She is holding my hand. My sister is holding my hand."

"Yes, my child. She remembers. The smallest kindness is never forgotten. And for that very reason I will hold your hand in mine. Never underestimate the power of prayer, my child. Now let's get a move on. We will get you settled in quickly because there is a long line-up forming at the Gate. Peter will be coming to me with complaints. He will be saying there is no rest for the wicked."

I had to laugh when I heard him say those words. "My Mom used to often complain there was no rest for the wicked."

"I know son. And she also told you to hold your sister's hand. Am I right?"

"Yes, Lord, you are absolutely right."

"If your mother were here now she would be telling you to take my hand. Do you believe that?"

"I do, sir."

"Then what are you waiting for? Take my hand child and let's get a move on."

***

THE HOLE IN THE WALL

Lucille packed all her clothes into green plastic garbage bags and fastened their tops with the white twist ties that came in the box with the bags. There were three bags in all not counting her two winter coats which, one at a time, she took off their wire hangers. It was not an easy task but she folded, pushed and prodded the knee-length blue polyester quilted coat into the cardboard box. On top of it she placed the easier to fold nylon ski jacket. She then sealed the sloping to the left top of the bulging box with the thin, beige, paper tape she had picked up at the Dollarama.

She remembered her daughter, Sara, asking, "If you are bound and determined to move north, why not just rent a little place, live in it for a year and see if you will even like living there?"

"I'll like it," Lucille had responded.

"But how can you consider buying a house on your tight budget, Mom?"

"I'll get my government cheque now that I'm sixty-five. The budget won't be as tight as it was. And I don't have to be in a hurry to pay my sister back for the down payment. I can spread it out and pay it along with the loan money."

"But I'm worried about you living alone in a town where you know nobody."

"I'll meet people."

"But you can't afford a house!"

"I'll get the supplement. I'll manage."

Lucille tried to lift the box of coats in order to carry it out to the truck parked in her daughter's big city driveway. It was heavier than she expected it to be.

With each step she took she slid the box along the bedroom floor with her feet which she noticed were still warmly wrapped in her slippers. She had forgotten she was wearing them and now it was too late to pack them.

Oh, Lordy, she thought, I hope I've left a pair of shoes out for me to wear. If they are already packed in the truck I will have to make the long drive and arrive at my new home in these scruffy bedroom slippers.

Her son-in-law, Martin Cooper, was going to drive the truck from Toronto to the small northern town. And he had generously offered to pay the gas expense too. His friend, Howard Langley, had offered to help with the move. Lucille was grateful to the two men and, although he had never said a word about it, she had a hunch Martin was grateful she was making this move. Not too many young men want an aging mother-in-law taking up space in their house these days.

At 65 years of age Lucille didn't feel old. Moving to a retirement town was the sensible thing to do. She had been living with Lucille and Martin for too long. When she had been of some use to them by looking after the grandchildren so they could both work she felt she was paying her way. But now the children were half-way through high school. They didn't need a baby-sitter anymore. *Or maybe they do, Lucille thought, but they sure don't want one.* When not in school seventeen-year-old Gordie spent all his time in the basement with his friends playing rock music while fifteen-year-old Gillian spent hours in front of the bathroom mirror fretting over a new pimple.

Lucille loved her grandchildren. She knew her love was returned and she would miss the kids but it was time for her to move along. Since her divorce seven years ago she had burned some bridges and now it was time to mend some fences. *Is sixty-five too old to start a new life for myself, she wondered.*

Her ex-husband died within two years after their separation and divorce. Of course with his love of women and good Canadian rye whiskey he left no money behind him when he went to meet his Maker. *He wouldn't have wanted to waste a penny on life insurance when the same money would buy a case of beer,* she thought as she stood in her daughter's doorway and watched the men load the truck with her few belongings.

She didn't own much anymore. She had either sold or given away most of what she had when she lost her secretarial job with the construction company and accepted the invitation to move in with her daughter six years ago. One result of this change of address was a downward slide from low income to no income. As a secretary in the small construction company in Metro

Toronto Lucille didn't earn a lot but it was enough to pay for her small studio apartment. When she lost this job the employment insurance just wasn't enough to meet her big city expenses. And she was only eligible to collect the insurance for a short period of time.

As hard as she worked on her job search no employer was eager to hire a fifty-nine-year-old no matter how skilled she was. Just like her ex-husband, these bosses wanted younger women who would do more to dress up the office with their good looks.

It was really out of the goodness of her heart that her daughter, Sara, insisted that the children needed their grandmother for after-school care. Martin made a living as a postal worker. Sara waitressed in order to bring a little extra money into the home. Lucille had no housing or food expenses but with no income she had no life outside the house. She couldn't afford a movie or a new dress. She was financially poor and as the years went by she was beginning to feel an emotional and a spiritual poverty as well.

During her years as a secretary in the Toronto construction industry Lucille had learned a lot about demographics. Throughout the recession housing starts were very slow. People couldn't afford to buy new homes and were challenged in the effort to provide basic necessities like food, clothing, heat and other utilities. Lucille had read that 10.8 percent of all Canadians, which at that time meant 3.4 million people, were eking out a living below the poverty line. It was only because Lucille had made the decision to move in with her daughter that she wasn't joining the thousands of others who were making frequent visits to food banks.

There was no pleasure in poverty. Now that the grandchildren were grown Lucille was aware that she had out-aged her usefulness. She had to do something.

Lucille had a sister, Karen, who had made different choices and who had made her career life one that achieved financial success. She was not a wealthy woman but she had enough money invested and saved that she was able to give Lucille the $2,000.00 she needed for a down payment on the old, small, northern town house. Lucille did not qualify for a traditional house mortgage. Instead Karen gave her sister the additional $48,000.00 in an interest-free loan to be repaid at the rate of $400.00 dollars per month.

Moving day had arrived.

Martin came into the house. "The truck is loaded," he said. "Anything more to go on the truck, Mom?"

Lucille had been smart enough to leave a pair of shoes out of the packing boxes. "Just these old slippers," she said. "But maybe I can just carry them in a bag."

"Give them to me. I'll find a spot for them in the back of the truck," he offered.

"Then I guess that's it. Guess I'm ready to go."

That's when Sara started to cry. Of course once she started Lucille could no longer contain her emotion. "I'll miss you, Sara. I know it's a long drive but I hope you and the kids can find a way to get up for some visits."

"You know we will, Mom."

It was a long drive. For more than five long hours Lucille sat scrunched on the truck's front seat between Martin who drove and Howard who, not blessed with the slightest musical talent, constantly sang along with the radio which blared because Martin was a little hard of hearing.

When they pulled into the driveway of the little bungalow Lucille's sigh of relief could have been heard by Sara in Toronto. "Thank you, boys," was all she said.

It was just past noon. While the men set to work unloading the truck Lucille was the cop who stood on the verandah and directed traffic. "That goes to the bedroom. You can leave that box in the living-room."

The men managed to get Lucille's double bed up. They hooked up the little TV set and they managed to get furniture into the room where it belonged. Sara had made a big bag of sandwiches and this is what they had for their dinner.

That night the men slept in Lucille's bed while she slept on the living-room couch.

There had been no time to unpack any boxes. When the men left early the next morning, Lucille stood amidst the chaos. Undaunted, she set to work.

Within three weeks Lucille had all the boxes unpacked. She had found a place for everything and being an organized woman Lucille knew how to keep everything in its place. Government cheques arrived. She was grateful for her old age pension with supplement and in addition to this she had a small monthly Canada Pension payment; a result of her many years working as a secretary.

Lucille's income as a senior citizen at that time was just under $1,000.00 a month. She made an agreement with her sister, Karen, to repay $100.00 a month on the $2,000.00 down payment plus $400.00 a month on the mortgage. This payment amounted to a little more than half her total monthly income.

Still Lucille was determined. Once she was settled in her house she began looking around for a part-time job but jobs of any kind were not in abundance in the small northern town and employers were not eager to hire a woman in her senior years despite her valid work experience.

The first couple of months she made her repayments okay. But the bills were arriving faster than she could have hoped. There was a charge for installation of the telephone that she hadn't counted on. The utility bills were higher than she had expected and though it was early fall the weather had turned very cool and the furnace started to kick in. Lucille had no idea heating bills could be so persistent.

During the years she had lived with her daughter, Lucille had no need to pay for her food. She was shocked to see how high food prices had risen and tried to put as little as possible into her grocery cart when she shopped. *I shouldn't eat so much anyway, she thought. It will do me good to lose a few pounds.*

With no friends in town and being so far from her family it wasn't long before Lucille began to withdraw into herself. She became afraid to venture out alone. She felt marginalized and isolated. Depression and anxiety increased when another month rolled around and she realized she did not have enough money to pay her mortgage.

Lucille knew that her sister would probably understand and give her a little more time to make the payment but Lucille also knew that if she began to fall behind she may never catch up.

Never a religious woman, Lucille, at her wits' end, turned to prayer. She got into the habit of spending time in her backyard where she would do a little weeding and watering of the existing flowers that had been planted by the home's previous owner. Once her gardening tasks were complete she would sit on a small wooden bench under the Lilac tree to rest. There was a large boulder on the ground beside the bench.

The mortgage payment was due in a few days. Lucille, in desperation, placed her hand on the rock and she prayed. *Dear God, you know my needs. Please help me.*

She felt a warm, powerful energy emanating from the rock. This energy travelled throughout her body and although she did not hear a voice, somehow she knew the words, *"Hole in the Wall."*

"You think this house is a hole in the wall, Lord?" she asked.

Hole in the wall was the only response.

Throughout that day Lucille fretted and worried. *I've been a fool to think I could pay for a house on my own.* Still she believed that if she could get through this month which held so many extra expenses because of the move that she would be all right. *Maybe I should call my sister and tell her I will be late with the payment this month.* But she didn't want to call her sister. She didn't want to fall behind.

That night she lay sleepless in her bed. She thought of her own mother who was a woman of strong faith. As a child when her mother was struggling to keep the family fed she would often say, "The Lord will provide."

These thoughts of her mother led Lucille to remember her answer to prayer that afternoon. *Some answer! Hole in the wall! Thanks for nothing, God!*

Hours passed. The morning sun was beginning to peek through the bedroom window and still Lucille had not slept. All she had been able to think about was what a fool she had been to think she would be able to pay for this hole in the wall all by herself. *Hole in the head is more like it!*

She got up from bed with her decision made. She would have a cup of coffee and then wait for a decent morning hour to call her sister and tell her she could not make a full payment on the mortgage this month. She could manage to pay her $200.00 but that would be $300.00 short of the required amount.

It was a beautiful bright fall morning. Lucille decided to carry her cup of coffee from the kitchen out into the backyard. Once again she sat on the bench beneath the tree. Once again she reached out, in a last ditch effort, for help. Coffee cup in one hand, with the other she placed it on the large boulder and prayed.

God answers every prayer.

The answer was *Hole in the Wall.*

Again she recalled her mother's strong faith. *I ask for financial help and God's answer is hole in the wall.* At once it dawned on her. Maybe the house is not a hole in the wall but maybe this house has a hole in a wall.

She began her search at the back of the house. She found nothing in the bedroom, the bathroom or the living room. It was a small house and this left only the tiny basement.

Down the stairs she went. It was an unfinished basement with poured concrete gray walls. To Lucille's dismay these walls had no holes in them. There was a small room partitioned off in the back of the basement. The former owner had used this room for growing plants in preparation before transferring them into the backyard garden once spring arrived. The walls in this room had no holes in them either. In fact they were covered with sheets of shiny tinfoil.

Lucille's eyes viewed an ugly room; one that did nothing to lift her spirits. Frustration found its way up through her body. To release the tension she made a fist and swung her right hand into the tinfoil. *I'll make a damn hole in the wall!*

Her solid punch tore the tinfoil making a hole. Lucille began tearing the tinfoil from the wall. As it landed in small heaps around her feet, for reasons she could not explain, she felt better; lighter; more like her old self.

Then it happened. A white envelope that had been hidden in the wall behind the tinfoil fluttered to the basement floor. *Probably an old love letter the old guy had hidden from his wife,* she thought.

She picked up the small, sealed envelope. Sinking to the floor she sat, prepared to read. When she opened the envelope she could not stop her tears.

In her hands she held three $100.00 bills.

Just enough; it was just enough. Why the money had been hidden, Lucille had no idea.

She sat on the floor and thanked God for the hole in the wall. She thought once again of her mother who had always believed that the Lord would provide.

As she made her way back upstairs, for the first time in what seemed a very long time, Lucille smiled.

A STRANGER IN A STRANGE LAND

I have never thought of myself as an advocate for the homeless. I can't say I was far removed from those living on the ragged edge of life but I can say I was at least a pay cheque away.

You can't live in Toronto and not be aware of homelessness but certainly I was never approached by beggars on the quiet residential street where I lived. Never, that is, until that day I met Alexander.

It was Christmas Eve morning. A light snowfall overnight covered the slush on the city sidewalk. I was walking down the street minding my own business as one learns it is wise to do in a big city. I was heading for the subway station on my way to work. I was less than a block away from home when from out of nowhere two dirty, stained, brown trouser legs with even dirtier large, bare feet extending from the tattered hems shot out from behind a snow glittery hedge.

I tripped and landed kerplunk on my knees on an icy patch on the sidewalk.

"Ow!" My pretty blue slacks were torn and just as I tried to stand up I noticed the bright red spots. I sat bottom on the ice while I rolled up the leg of my slacks. "Ow!" I shouted again, this time even louder when I saw all the blood trickling down the front of my leg. I am a person with a very sensitive stomach. I cannot bear the sight of blood; especially when it is my own.

Then I heard a deep, masculine voice. "Sorry lady, I didn't see you coming."

I gazed at the two large bare feet on the snowy sidewalk. I followed my gaze up the long length of the trouser legs to the point where they met the red windburned upper body of a man whose chest was as naked as his feet. "Good grief! You must be freezing!"

At once I recognized the synergy between the homeless man and the sidewalk. It was like he belonged there and I was the intruder. I lifted myself up from the sidewalk, bent over and rolled my pants leg back down so that the dripping blood was mostly hidden from view. I could not go to work in this condition. My plan was to go back home, clean and bandage my cut, call in to work, get changed and then set off once more.

"I didn't see you coming," he repeated. "I really am sorry my big feet got in your way."

His sincere apology stopped me in my tracks. I permitted my eyes to land on the boyish, thin, blue-eyed face; its chin covered in light blond stubble and its head crowned with thick, dirty blond hair. He looked pathetic but harmless enough.

"It's okay," I replied. "It was an accident."

"Thanks," he said as he sneaked quick glances at my face. I noticed he wasn't able to look me straight in the eye.

"What are you doing here anyway?" I asked. "Were you sleeping behind that hedge?"

"Yes, ma'am."

"And there you stay with no shoes, no jacket, no ….."

"Yes, ma'am, no nothing!"

"You're homeless?"

He surprised me by saying, *"The foxes have holes and the birds in the sky have nests, but the Son of Man has no place to lay his head."*

Something kept me planted there on that sidewalk. "Are you a poet?"

And he laughed. "I'm no poet. That was a quotation. Do you know who said those words?"

"You just did," I countered.

He laughed again and his beautiful smile was sunshine for my soul. It was spoiled only by a most dreadful halitosis which was inescapable even though I was now standing a few feet from him. "That was a quotation from the Bible," he told me. "Those are words that Jesus said in the Book of Luke, chapter nine."

"You know your Bible then?"

"Yes, ma'am. I'm a stranger in a strange land but I'm no stranger to the Bible.

"Well, I should know better than to be talking to a stranger."

"Do not forget to entertain strangers for by so doing some people have entertained angels without knowing it."

I was impressed. "I suppose that's from the Bible too?"

"Yes, ma'am."

"Are you some kind of a Jesus freak or something?"

"No, ma'am, just an ordinary freak but in spite of it all, I do have a strong faith in God. Besides it's Christmas!"

"Does the freak have a name and how old are you anyway?

"My name is Alexander and I'm twenty-one, ma'am."

Just a boy, I realized with a new understanding of why he kept calling me ma'am. I had recently turned twenty-seven and I guess in his eyes I was way over the proverbial hill. "When's the last time you had something to eat?" I asked.

He lowered his head and in a soft voice said, "I don't remember, ma'am."

"So are you an angel, Alexander?"

"Ma'am?"

"Didn't I hear you say that some people have entertained angels without knowing it?"

"That's what we are told Jesus said. *Love ye therefore the stranger for ye were strangers in the land of Egypt.*"

I had to laugh out loud and the laughter felt good. It was something I hadn't done a lot of lately. I was always the dependable, serious one; head down, going to and from a job that did nothing to excite me, returning from work to an apartment that was often a lonely place to be.

"I don't know if I will learn to love you, Alexander, but I can offer you some breakfast."

"Breakfast, ma'am?"

"I live just down the street. I need to get home to fix up this knee before I can get to work. I'm already late so a little bit later won't make that big a difference. I'll cook you up some bacon and eggs and maybe you can tell me what happened to your clothes and where are your shoes? I thought *all God's chillun got shoes."*

"I know that song. *When I get to Heaven gonna put on my shoes; gonna walk all over God's heaven"*

Alexander had a beautiful soft tenor voice. Listening to him sing I wanted to pick up my guitar. For a few weeks I'd been taking lessons and I knew how to play a few chords. He stopped singing when I told him I liked his voice.

"I like to sing," was all he said.

We climbed the stairs up to my apartment. I unlocked my door and invited him in.

"I was a stranger and you took me in," he recited.

I cleaned my wound, applied a Band-Aid. It had long stopped bleeding and I could see that it was a minor injury but my good blue slacks were beyond repair. I changed into a navy pair. Returning to my living room I smiled at Alexander who remained seated on the couch.

I was acting totally out of what I thought was my character. And I was enjoying myself doing so. "By the way Alexander, my name is Kate. Do you want to take a shower while I cook you up some breakfast?"

"A shower? It's a long time since I had a shower."

"You go ahead. Use the bath towel on the rack and if you look in the little cupboard under the bathroom sink you will find a bottle of Scope. Please use it."

"It's that bad, is it?" he asked, his words creeping through his embarrassment.

"No, it's worse!"

"Guess I'm in pretty bad shape, Kate."

I was just plating the bacon and sunny-side-up eggs when Alexander came back into the living-room. Still no shoes, no shirt but his skin was smooth, sleek and shiny clean. The little girl in my heart could not help but notice that he was attractive.

I sat across the dining table from him and watched him eat. "What happened to your shoes and shirt, Alexander? How could you survive this cold weather without a jacket or a coat?"

"The old shirt just plumb wore out, Kate. And some time back somebody stole my jacket. The shoes were stolen night before last."

I didn't want to cry but tears dripped from my eyes of their own volition. I felt more aware than I had in a very long time of how much I take for granted in my life. I have a job, a home, and good health. I have a wardrobe full of clothes and I have a good mind that is overflowing with thoughts and ideas.

"How did you get into such a state, Alexander?"

"It's a long story, Kate."

Already I was more than an hour late for work. I still had not called my boss to explain my tardiness. "I have time to listen but I have to make a quick call first."

Returning to the living-room I felt as though an unknown burden had been lifted. I removed Alexander's empty plate from the table and poured coffee into two mugs.

He told me about his life growing up in a small northern town. He talked about his mother who passed away from cancer when he was eleven and how his father did his best to raise him on his own. With his dad away at work much of the time he drew within himself and became what most would call a loner. Missing his mother, he took to reading her Bible. From an early age he was proficient at memorizing verses. Somehow quoting from the Bible helped him to feel closer to her. He graduated high school and began looking for a job.

"Jobs were scarce in my home town, Kate. When I turned nineteen I came to Toronto in search of work. I paid the price for some dumb decisions. The little money I had soon disappeared. That's when I began doing a little singing for my supper. I always liked to sing and I discovered that there was always someone willing to put a Looney into my cap. I've been doing this for a couple years now. Then my cap was stolen while I was asleep in a store doorway one night. When my shoes and jacket were stolen from me I was in no shape to sing for my supper. I was just too cold. I didn't know where to turn. I was afraid the cops would pick me up so I knew I had to get off Yonge Street. That's why I chose this street last night. I decided to sleep behind the tall hedge. I thought it would be safer and the hedge provided some warmth."

I had no words for him when he finished his story. I got up from the table, walked over and grabbed my guitar. "I'm just learning to play this thing," I told him, as I strummed a few chords. "Sing a song for me, Alex?"

"Here's one my mother taught me, Kate. It's a song by Harry Connick Jr. and it goes something like this. In his beautiful tenor tones he began to sing, *People with hope have a special prayer, a louder drum, a brighter flare. This is a song for the hopeful. May God hear it sung.*

I didn't know the song but I followed along the best I could with the guitar.

And this is how Alexander and I came to be friends. His friendship is the greatest Christmas gift I have ever received. Meeting him changed the direction not only of Alexander's life but that of my own.

Sure there were challenges to overcome but from that evening onward Alexander stayed with me. I bought him a warm jacket for our first Christmas together. With a shirt on his back and good shoes on his feet very early in the new year he found a salesman's job in a department store.

In the evenings we practiced our music. My guitar playing improved and Alex had the voice of an angel.

These were the humble beginnings of *Kate and Alex.*

We have an agent now. We have a lot of gigs scheduled and life is good. We hope to have children one day. Will I teach my children not to talk to strangers? Maybe. Maybe not.

This story I've told you all took place two years ago. And now it is another Christmas Eve. Alex and I are honoured to be here on this beautiful evening to entertain you.

I am warmed by the applause of the audience.

"Alex, come on out onto the stage with me and let's give these good people what they have been waiting to hear." I announce as I begin to strum my old guitar.

Alex joins me on the stage. "Merry Christmas everyone!" he shouts.

While I play he thrills the audience with his

version of Harry Connick Jr.'s 'Song for the Hopeful.'

He makes the song his own.

*There's a song for the doubtful. There's a song for the
lost. There's a song for the desert barren but crossed.
But for those who are strong of spirit, maybe they don't
need to hear it. But still a song for them, a simple song
for them. Well, nothing can change a season's soul.
It's all in the love that makes it whole. This is a song
for the hopeful.*

RUNNING ON EMPTY

My name is Ralph Morton. I'm an ordinary man and I am not given to flights of fancy. People who know me will tell you that I am not the kind of person who puts a lot of faith in fantastic reporting. I'm a down to earth guy and I don't have a wild imagination.

It broke my heart when my best mate Gerry was killed by a falling tree this morning. Gerry was a lumberjack and he worked in the bush north of my small northern town. I first met Gerry when I signed a contract with the company where he works as a lumberjack. It was then that I began hauling the logs in my old truck to the sawmill where they cut the logs into lumber.

It was a tragic accident. Gerry was good at his job but today his number was up. The falling tree hit him on the side of his head and knocked him to the ground. I just happened to be there and I saw it happen. I ran as fast as I could and was the first to reach my buddy. Blood was trickling from beneath his wet brown hair and down the side of his face but he was conscious and able to speak.

"Hang in there, good buddy," I told him. "Help is on its way."

"Ralph, Ralph," he whispered.

"Yes, Gerry, I'm here with you."

"Ralph, find the Barken Tree. It will solve all your problems."

"Yeah, sure, buddy," I answered. I figured the knock on the head had made my friend delusional. I mean everybody knows there is no such thing as a tree that barks.

"I've been looking for a while, Ralph. I know I was almost there. Find the Barken Tree, promise?"

"Sure, Gerry, I promise," I said. The ambulance arrived then and the paramedics lifted my friend onto a stretcher. I was later told he died before they reached the hospital.

Gerry had become my best mate and it broke my heart when he passed. That night, after hauling the logs to the mill, I drove my old truck home to the small townhouse where I lived with my wife, Laura. I was two weeks away from pay day and my old truck was running on fumes. It seemed to me that my whole life was running on empty.

We were luckier than some to live in an end unit which meant we had a private driveway. I backed the truck into the dirt drive and parked. Laura was a stickler for clean floors. She had me better trained than our old dog, Max, used to be so I knew enough to always come into the house using the back door. I missed Max. He was a faithful and a loving pet but the day came when Laura insisted he had to go. "I can't stand the dog hair all over the place and his muddy paw prints are driving me up the wall."

It hurt to let the good fellow go. I found consolation when another good friend offered to take him in. I missed living with Max but appreciated the evenings when I could drive to my friend's place and visit Max for a while.

From the day of our wedding twenty-four years ago Laura kept a tidy house. From the word go she made it her life's passion to break me of all my bad and messy habits. Boots off before I come in the back door; cigarette smoking outside in the back yard no matter what the weather; and if I make a mess I better be quick to grab the broom, the cloth, the vacuum cleaner or whatever it took to clean up that mess.

Laura had always been the same way with the kids. Together we raised two boys, Raymond and Reuben, who couldn't wait to get away from home when they started college in the nearest big centre. Today their dorm rooms are a pig sty and they are ecstatic in their sloppiness as they study subjects they will never, in my opinion, be able to use in real life. In spite of their sloth both boys have somehow developed an air about them; almost an arrogance. They look down on me and Laura because we have no college diplomas hanging on the wall.

Laura and me, we didn't have the money and we couldn't afford to pay the boys' way through school. I figure by the time they are both ready to haul wood they will be snowed under by student loans. Both boys say they will never drive truck. Ray has his mind set on working as an accountant for the government and Reuben tells us he plans to teach literature. Good luck to them with their highfalutin dreams and goals. I used to have some dreams myself but that was a long time ago.

Today I'm surprised I can still move my legs. They are stuck in the same rut as everything in my life seems to be.

I came into the house. It was as usual neat as a button. I walked across the kitchen floor in my socks and called out, "I'm home, Laura."

I noticed there were pots bubbling on the stove and the kitchen table was set for two. Everything in Laura's life had to be perfect. And of course because it wasn't or, better put, because I wasn't perfect that made me the source of Laura's ongoing discontent. I was convinced that she was on the verge of a meltdown every time I came into the house and today was no exception.

I found her in the living room. She was polishing the already shining coffee table. "I'm home, Laura," I called again.

Cloth in hand she rubbed faster; she rubbed harder. "Table's filthy! Can't get these stains off!"

I approached her and reached out to take the cloth from her hand. "The table is beautiful, Laura. Clean and beautiful."

That's when she broke down. She sank onto the living room couch and I watched as her skin crinkled up and tears covered her face like a blanket. I put my arms around her and hid her sobs in my flannel checked shirt. "It's okay, Laura. I'm home now."

I felt smaller than a cent and just as useless. I knew it was my fault that Laura's world had shrunk to pea size. I never earned enough money to move us into a nicer place. When I first met Laura it was years ago in Toronto. She was raised in a nice home and was used to having the finer things in life.

From the time she married me and moved to this small northern town her hopes and dreams began dying their slow and painful death. After the birth of our second son, Reuben, she seemed to fall apart. She spent too much time weeping and worrying.

At that time the doctor told us that Laura was suffering from post-partum psychosis. "It's better known as postpartum blues, Ralph," the doctor explained. "Give it some time. It will pass."

The thing is though that with Laura it didn't pass. Sure, she did her best to hide what was happening to her.   She was irritable and I never knew what I was coming home to because Laura had these extreme mood swings.   Maybe I should have sought better treatment for her but if I ever mentioned seeing a psychiatrist to Laura she would either burst into tears or she would pick up the frying pan and threaten to whack me upside the head.

It's no wonder the boys couldn't wait to leave home though Laura was always a good mother.   She loved her boys but it was Laura who planted the seeds of better things in the heads of my boys.   I think it is her doing that I have two sons on a beer budget with champagne taste.

Once Laura's tears stopped flowing we made our way into the kitchen where she served me a lovely supper.   Laura was an excellent cook and she kept a spotless clean home.   When alone she achieved these things while keeping her emotions bottled and her feelings drawn tighter than a drum. She made me promise that I would never take her to a mental hospital.

All these years I've kept my promise even though I'm not sure it is one I should have made. And now over supper I told Laura about the death of my friend Gerry.

Her response was, "He is better off now. I will be better off when I die too."

"Don't talk like that, Laura," I begged. "I love you and I need you in my life."

That's when she burst into tears again. "I'm trying, Ralph. God knows I'm trying."

"I know you are, Laura. Don't cry. Everything is going to be okay."

When I lay in bed that night I could not get Gerry off my mind. I remembered his words, "Ralph, find the Barken Tree. It will solve all your problems." And when I finally slept that night I dreamed a dream. In my dream I saw a tree; one that was unique in that its flowers never failed to bloom regardless of the weather. The multi-coloured flowers bloomed throughout the unpredictable spring temperatures, throughout the heat of summer, the relief of autumn and the ice of winter.

These flowers had a fragrance that reminded me of cinnamon toast. This tree was verisimilar. It appeared to be real and once I experienced this dream I made a vow that I would keep my promise to Gerry. I would find the Barken Tree. I wasn't sure how finding it would solve my problems but I determined to find out.

I awakened the following morning to find Laura in a very cheerful mood. I can't say I ever became accustomed to her mood swings but I always filled with gratitude when she was in a good mood. "I made you cinnamon toast for breakfast," she announced.

Immediately I thought again of the Barken Tree and its aromatic blossoms that reminded me of cinnamon toast. Should I tell Laura about this tree? No, I decided. The search for the Barken Tree will be one for me alone.

That morning I drove the old truck to Canadian Tire where I had the tank filled. I hated to put it on the credit card but I had no other source of funds. Once the truck was gassed up I pulled back onto the highway and headed north.

When I reached the lumberjack camp I got out of the truck and rather than starting to load right away I walked over to the spot where the following morning

Gerry had lain. "I've been looking for a while, Ralph. I know I was almost there," I remembered him saying.

I looked around me. Keeping the vivid dream picture in mind I began walking. That morning I spent a good hour walking and searching for the Barken Tree with no success. I returned to my truck and with the help of another fellow there we loaded up my old truck for another delivery of logs to the sawmill.

A few days later I attended the funeral of my good buddy Gerry. While the minister recited his prayers I renewed my promise to continue to search for the Barken Tree.

One evening I visited Raymond and Reuben in their shared dormitory room. It was Reuben who was studying Literature and hoped to be a writer and a professor one day. "Reuben, have you ever heard of the word Barken before?"

"Sure," he answered.

"Well, what does it mean, son?"

"It's a word I've seen in some poetry, Dad, though it's not commonplace. It simply means something made of bark."

"Have you ever heard of a Barken Tree, Reuben?"

"Well, no, Dad, but I mean all trees have bark on their trunks, eh?"

"Yes, yes, that's true enough, son. Thanks."

Call me a fool but in my mind a man's word is his bond. I may not be very wise in the choice of promises I make in life. I often question the wisdom of keeping my promise to my wife. She would probably benefit from visits with a psychiatrist or even a hospital stay. But a promise is a promise. And my promise to

Gerry on his earthly deathbed was one I was determined to keep as well even though I'm sure people must have thought I was nuts making those long walks every morning through the woods.

"I'm trying to lose a few pounds," I lied to anyone who asked me why I spent so much time wandering through the forest each work day morning.

Three weeks after the death of my good buddy I made the discovery. I had walked for about two hours that morning journeying due north from the spot where Gerry lay on the ground that fateful day. Suddenly I smelled a fragrance that reminded me of cinnamon. I followed my nose until there, almost hidden, in the midst of a grove of Maples was a small cluster of several Barken Trees.

They appeared just as I had seen them in my dream. Each tree had an abundance of multi-coloured blossoms. The tiny fragrant flowers had petals of blue, red, orange and yellow. I could scarcely believe my eyes. Like I told you I am not given to flights of fancy. I don't have a wild imagination. What I was seeing this morning was real.

I remembered Gerry telling me that finding the Barken Tree would solve my problems. Now that I had finally found it I wasn't sure what I was supposed to do. I wasn't sure how this discovery would solve my problems but I determined to find out.

I didn't want to kill a tree so I decided that I would not pull one from the earth or chop one down. What I did decide to do was to fill my pocket with some of the Barken Tree's flowers.

That day I walked back to my truck. I loaded it with logs and made my daily trip to the sawmill before returning home with the pocket filled with flowers. I found Laura asleep on the living-room couch when I entered the house. Years of experience told me that this meant she had not had a good day.

Without waking her I went into the kitchen. I removed the flowers from my pocket and reaching up into one of the kitchen cupboards I retrieved a see-through freezer bag. I put the flowers into this bag. I was about to put the bag into the cupboard when on impulse I decided to see what kind of a tea I could make with these flowers. I really have no idea what possessed me to do this but I admit to having a strong sense of the presence of my friend Gerry there with me. I rinsed the teapot with hot water at the sink. I filled and plugged in our electric kettle. Not sure how much to use I decided on one teaspoonful of flowers in the pot before I poured the boiling water over them.

The lovely fragrance of cinnamon filled the kitchen. I poured just a little of the tea into a cup and tasted it. I was very happy to discover that it tasted as good as it smelled. It was a beautiful cinnamon tea although as soon as I had that thought I corrected it. "This is a beautiful Barken Tea," I said aloud to no one there.

I drank the tea. Within just a few minutes I felt myself relaxing. I felt the stress and the worries of my life depart leaving me with a new feeling of confidence and pleasure.

In that moment of relaxation I felt the warm friendship of my friend Gerry as it wrapped itself around my shoulders. "Find the Barken Tree and it will solve all your problems," he had told me moments before his death.

"Thank you, Gerry." Even though I whispered I believed that he could hear me.

I proceeded to take another teacup from the shelf and this time with it a saucer. Laura would never drink tea from a cup without a saucer. I poured a cup of the fragrant Barken Tea for my wife and I carried it to her where she lay on the couch.

I reached out and caressed her shoulder. "Wake up, Laura. I'm home."

She opened her blue eyes. I could see the fear resting in those eyes. As I assisted her to sit up on the couch I could feel the stress and the taut nerves in her body. "I made you a cup of tea, Laura."

She didn't say anything but she did take the cup and saucer from me. As she took the first sip of her tea I prayed. I prayed harder and more sincerely than I had ever prayed in my life. Laura drank her tea. And when it was finished she smiled. I couldn't remember the last time I had seen my wife smile. She smiled and she said, "What lovely tea. Thank you, Ralph."

From that day forward I made my wife a cup of Barken Tea every day when I returned from work. Within a very short time Laura's mood swings disappeared.

I began to take a thermos of tea with me when I went to visit my sons Raymond and Reuben. Soon I began to notice very positive changes in their attitude and their behaviour. They began making regular phone calls to their mother and of course these calls further improved Laura's approach to life.

I drank the tea on a regular basis myself and in what seemed like no time at all my outlook on life improved. I began to feel like less of a loser. I began to believe that my life did have value and I was someone to be respected and treated well in life.

I knew that I needed to inform someone in authority about the value of the Barken Tree. Its gifts would be of value to many in our world; especially those who, like my Laura, have suffered from sometimes debilitating mood swings. Yes, I knew I could not keep this secret to myself but before I made that life-changing phone call I dug up a good plot of land in my backyard. I drove again to the Maple Grove and this time, rather than just taking a few flowers from a tree and filling my pocket, I dug up four of the several trees there. I brought these four trees home with me and I replanted them in my backyard.

No longer do I feel like my life is running on empty. Today, thanks to Gerry and his message; thanks to the blossoms of the Barken Tree my cup is full and running over with blessings. People who know me will tell you that I am not the kind of person who puts a lot of faith in fantastic reporting. I'm a down to earth guy and I don't have a wild imagination. I am not imagining the beautiful smile on my Laura's face each day. These things I have told you are not only verisimilar; they are absolutely true. My name is Ralph Morton. I'm an ordinary man not given to flights of fancy.

ANOTHER MOTHER'S DAY

Tony's phone call planted the idea. "He's either drunk or crazy," my sister Molly insisted when I told her what he had said. "Anyway how come he phoned you and not me?"

"I don't know. Maybe he did phone you. You're such a gadabout! Maybe you weren't home when he called you."

"He could have left a message."

"Really? Tell me you're joking! You really think he would leave a traceable message like that?"

"Okay, okay, so what did you say to him?"

"I told him to go back to bed. But he told me he was coming over here this afternoon to talk about it, Molly. That's why I wanted you to be here."

My sister's pretty face slumped like a faded flower. Molinda is the baby of the family and I don't feel good about dragging her into this crazy scheme but somehow I knew this was something where she could not be left out the way she often was by me and Tony when we were all kids.

Although Molly to this day doesn't believe it, Anthony and I didn't leave her out to hurt her. We knew she was hurt enough by our nut case of a mother just like we all were. No, we purposely tried to leave her out of a lot of things in order to help protect her. To understand what I mean you would have had to know Francis, our mother.

One of my earliest memories is being dragged by the arm along Toronto's hot city sidewalk by my mother, Francis Matheson. "Hurry up, Paulette!" she muttered as she increased her pace leaving my four year old legs weak and sore. I remember falling to the

213

cement scraping my knee then hastening to stand because my dear mother, Francis, was not going to slow her gait. "We are going to be late for church!" she shouted. Then, "Now look what you've done, you clumsy child. You are getting blood on your best dress. I'll never get that out in a month of Sundays."

Her roughness hurt a lot when she dabbed the tissues against my injured knee. "Bloody stupid child!" she shouted throwing the red Kleenex into the gutter. "I'm already late for church and you are making me even later. I should have left you at home in the closet!"

Yes, I remember being four years old. I was an only child then therefore all my dear mother's fits of frustration were heaped solely upon me. I don't know where my father was. At that time I didn't even know who my father was.

I was five years old when my mother's fat belly collapsed and Anthony Matheson entered my world kicking and screaming. It was as though he knew the kind of home he was being born into, poor little fellow, and he didn't want to stay. I decided I would take care of Anthony and do my best to protect him from my mother's anger.

In no time at all or so it seemed my mother's belly grew fat again. This time it was my baby sister Molinda who arrived in need of my protection. "Don't cry little Molly. I'll take care of you," I promised.

When three year old Tony dropped the jam jar and turned the grey linoleum a bright red, I quickly dropped to my knees and began picking up the sticky glass pieces.

"Damn clumsy girl! Get into the closet and stay there until I tell you to come out!" she screamed. I did as my mother ordered. I was a big girl now, ten years old. I was well practiced at spending alone time in the front hall closet where I scrunched myself into a ball below the hems of mother's coats and jackets. Soon I would be way too big to take up closet space. I wondered where she would put me then.

I wasn't always able to protect my little brother and sister. Huddled in the coat closet I could hear the crack of my mother's large hand upon the faces of the little ones. Tony was stoic. He stayed quiet and allowed his mind to imagine how he would get his revenge. Molly was just the opposite and as I listened to her sobs and sighs I could literally feel my heart hardening.

In this way our childhood years passed. Tony, Molly and me: we were a tough trio but even together we were no match for our mother's unforgiving, damning ways. We never met our father. The only father we ever heard about was when Francis forced us to our knees to repeat *Our Father who art in heaven*, the Lord's Prayer. We often had to recite this prayer after a severe and cruel punishment at the hands of our mother.

Our dear mother always hammered it into our heads that our penance was just. She was always teaching us a lesson.

The older I became the more often I wished I could wave a magic wand to make my mother un-pretzeled. But my wish never became reality and throughout our childhood my mother remained twisted, complicated and plain downright abusive and mean.

Somehow Tony, Molly and me survived our childhood. We each got a job and moved out of our mother's house as soon as we finished high school. I was lucky to land a position in the office of a construction company. When Tony turned eighteen the company owner accepted my recommendation and took my brother on as a labourer. My little sister Polly began clerking in one of the city's well-known department stores.

Although none of us had a college education we were smart. More important than being intelligent was the fact that we were each motivated to make something of ourselves; to make our lives a success in order to ensure that we would stay out of our mother's house. I stayed with the same construction company for several years. I learned a lot on the job and by the time I was thirty years old I was an estimator. I was the one who put together the bids and most of my bids were successful and brought jobs to the company. I was doing okay and I was earning enough money to easily carry the mortgage on my own condo townhouse.

Tony was twenty-five and, no longer a labourer, he was foreman on a major construction site. At twenty-three Molinda now took care of the department store employees' payroll. She had progressed beyond working on the floor of the store. She was promoted and began working in the store's head office. She worked hard and was on her way up in the world she was creating for herself. Both Anthony and Molly now had their own apartments. In spite of or maybe because of our chaotic childhood the three of us worked hard and we were able to provide for ourselves the security and safety we had always craved yet never experienced as kids.

Yes, Tony, Molly and I remained a tough trio. Not a week went by without the three of us getting together. We practically never visited our mother Francis who remained a religious addict with the mouth of a drunken sailor. On the rare occasions when we did visit we would make sure the three of us arrived at her house together. It would be maybe at Christmas or on a Mother's Day. It didn't matter when it was. Always she would begin her diatribe. "If it wasn't for you damn kids I could have had a good life. Lazy, good-for-nothing brats you were, every bloody one of you! Ungrateful little bastards! Now I'm here all by myself with all my good years behind me; wasted. Yes, my life has been a total waste because of you lot holding me back; always there wanting more, more and more. I did everything for you and for what? For nothing, that's what for!"

"Yeah, sure Fran. Happy Mother's Day or Merry Christmas or Happy Birthday!" It was only on one of these society-determined special occasions that we three would force ourselves to darken our dear mother's doorway.

And now it was soon to be Mother's Day once again. Tony's phone call planted the idea. "He's either drunk or crazy, Polly," my sister Molly insisted when I told her what he had said.

"Well, he will be here any minute now, Molinda. We will soon see how drunk he is."

Rinnnnng! Rinnnnng!

"That's him now, Molly."

I opened the door and greeted my big little brother, Anthony. I felt his great arms around me and I melted in his warm hug. I smelled no liquor. I heard nothing but his soft, *hi sis.*

"Hi Tony, come on in. Molinda is already here."

In the living-room I watched as Molly and Tony shared a bear hug. Yes, our sick, twisted mother created chaotic suffering throughout our childhood years but more importantly her abuse drew the three of us closer together. We are strong allies against the dominant Francis.

"Will I make some coffee?" I asked.

"Sounds good," Tony smiled.

He followed me as I made my way to the kitchen and Molly wasn't far behind him. I made a pot of coffee and the three of us sat at my kitchen table hot mugs in hand. Tony told us about his idea.

"Oh, my god," Molly exclaimed. "How did you ever come up with such a great idea?"

"I've been planning revenge for years," Tony answered. "It's taken a long time to figure out exactly how we could successfully get away with giving her exactly what she deserves."

"I think you've nailed it, Tony." Molly was excited.

"Do you want to go ahead with Tony's plan?" I asked.

"Absolutely. There is no doubt in my mind."

"I don't know you two; this is very extreme."

"And locking you in a coat closet for half your life wasn't extreme?" Tony shouted.

"Pouring scalding water on Tony's hand when he dropped his cookie and left crumbs on the floor wasn't extreme?" Molly yelled.

Then I remembered seeing pretty little Molinda having her panties pulled down and being whipped until her tender bottom was red with welts from the ruler slapping over and over again because she didn't want to eat her vegetables.

"I'm in," I assured my brother and sister.

"Way to go, sis!" Tony shouted.

"Calm down, Tony," I cautioned. "We don't want my neighbours to hear of our plan."

"Does that mean that we are all in?"

"I'm in," Molly said.

"I'm in, yes," I repeated. "But it needs to happen here at my place. I'm the only one with a basement."

A week later it was Mother's Day once again. For the first time we had a plan for a big surprise celebration.

Fran accepted the invitation to come to my place for a luncheon on Mother's Day Sunday. Anthony and Molinda had been here for more than two hours at the time she arrived. They were kept busy arranging and keeping everything quiet in the basement so that she wouldn't suspect anything but the two came upstairs once our dear mother was seated in my living-room.

Before Anthony sat down in the easy chair across from the couch where Fran was sitting he walked across the room, bent down and checked to make sure the floor vent was wide open.

Molly sat beside our mother while I sat in the other occasional chair across from them. Tony spoke first. "Happy Mother's Day!" he shouted.

Mother was obviously surprised and taken aback by his friendly words. "Happy Mother's Day!" Molinda shouted. Smiling, I shouted the same before pouring the green tea into the four cups on the coffee table. Lifting one cup and saucer from the table I handed it to Fran. "I hope you enjoy this cup of tea, mother."

I passed the other cups and saucers to my brother and sister before placing one on the end table beside the chair where I once again sat down. The three of us made no motion to drink our tea but to Fran I said, "Lunch will soon be ready. Enjoy your tea, mother."

All three of us watched as she took the first sip. "What are you ingrates up to?" she suddenly demanded.

We just smiled.

Mother lifted her teacup and sipped. She was about to take another sip but then changed her mind. Putting the cup back in its saucer she screamed, "Are you trying to poison me?"

"Now mother," Tony responded, "why would we think of doing such a thing?"

"Drink your tea, mother," Molinda encouraged.

"Yes, enjoy your tea," I agreed. "I made green tea especially for you. I know it is your favourite."

"You bloody no-good pieces of shit! I know you are up to something. If you weren't so big now I'd lift my ruler and tan your asses. If you weren't so big I'd stuff you all into the closet like I did when you were little and I hope you would rot there once and for all. Have you poisoned this tea you lousy, ungrateful, bastards?"

"You can come up now!" Anthony shouted.

"I can come up where?" mother demanded.

Within short minutes my living-room was filled with women, all members of mother's Gospel Church choir. The expressions on their faces were priceless. Mother's mouth stayed wide open as she stared into the face of her friends' condemnation.

Molly and I kept busy with our cameras. We didn't want to miss a word, a sound, a look of dismay, of judgment or of fear.

This day was the first time Anthony, Molinda and I had a plan to surprise Francis Matheson on Mother's Day and yes, it was the last. The memory of this day is enough to keep us all smiling forever.

JACOB'S SEVEN LETTERS

I am Jacob Tyndal, the son of Marie and Thomas Tyndal. I spent my growing up years in a small northern town called Monteith. I never knew my mother. She died July 9, 1942 on the day I was born.

My father was employed by the Ministry of Community Safety and Correctional Services in the Monteith Correctional Complex in Iroquois Falls, a small town on the banks of the Abitibi River in Northern Ontario. Grandma Ellie told me that before he took on that job he was a young farmer who was good at working with the animals but when his young wife died he floundered.

"Sure, he lost a lot of money, Jacob, but worse than that he lost his will to live and this wasn't something he could borrow from a bank. Tom was a lost soul," Grandma said.

I don't remember anything about life on the farm but Gram told me that's because I spent very little time there with my father. My Grandma Ellie was a widow who lived alone in a little white frame house in Monteith. It was she who carried me, the newborn, from the hospital to her home.

Throughout the first two years of my life my only contact with my father was when every second weekend Gram would take me to his farm. I wish I could remember those visits.

When the farm sold my father started working at the Monteith Correctional Complex. He moved into the only rooming house in town just a few houses away from my Grandma's little house so by the time I was three I was able to visit with him more often. I remember holding Gram's hand and being led up the creaky steps to the second floor. I remember Gram knocking on the brown door while I stood beside her on the landing. I remember my father opening his door and saying, "Hello son". I wish I could remember him lifting me up into his arms but I don't.

I came home from school one afternoon when I was seven. The quiet scared me.

"Gram, I'm home. Where are you?"

Gram was always home when I returned from school. She was the only constant in my life. Gram was the one who loved me. She sent me to school with clean clothes and a sharp mind that wanted to learn. She took me to the Baptist Church Sunday School classes where I learned all about another Jacob who went to sleep with his head on a stone and dreamed of a ladder upon which angels of God were ascending and descending from Heaven.

I remember asking Grandma Ellie, "Gram, am I named after this Jacob in the Bible?

"I don't know, son," Gram replied. "But throughout the time your mother carried you inside her womb she would tell everyone that little Jacob would soon arrive."

When I discovered that it was my mother who had given me my name and when I learned the story of Jacob's stone pillow, the two happenings somehow melded and, though I did not understand why, stones became very important to me.

"Gram, where are you?" I shouted that world-changing day.

When I couldn't find her I went next door. My neighbor took me in her car to the hospital in Iroquois Falls where I saw my father. He was bent over in a waiting room chair. I saw his shoulders shaking. Fear filled my body.

"Where's Gram?"

My father raised his head. I saw his tear-soaked face. I pounded his arm and shouted, "Where's Gram?"

"She paid her dues, son. A better mother never lived."

"Where is she?" I demanded.

"She's gone, son, just like my father, my wife, and my farm. It's my punishment. I was not a good husband. I was not a good son. Now everything that ever mattered to me in my life is gone!"

"I'm still here, dad," I whispered through my seven-year-old tears. "Don't I matter?"

I guess he didn't hear me.

When my Grandma died I began to collect stones. I would never allow my stone collection to become larger than seven because at that age I began to live full time with my father. The number seven symbolized transformation; a step into an unknown way of life; a step back into the memories of two women who had loved me. In some strange fashion the seven stones formed the steps in Jacob's ladder connecting me to my mother and my grandmother in Heaven.

As a lonely child I would place one of my stones under my pillow hoping I would dream of Jacob's ladder. I dreamed it would take me up to Heaven where my mother and my dear Grandma Ellie lived.

Throughout my childhood journey I would keep an eye open and sometimes it would happen that a stone called out to me. Before I could make a decision to pick it up and accept it into my collection I struggled with the decision as to which stone I would have to let go. Letting go was a very hard thing for me to do.

When Grandma Ellie died my father packed up his few belongings and moved into her house to take care of me. Each week day I would go off to school. My dad would go off to work in the Monteith Correctional Complex. Because he was good at working with animals he was given the job of looking after the animals that the prison officials believed assisted in rehabilitating the prisoners.

The Great War had been over for five years the year my Dad moved into Gram's house to look after me. I craved closeness with my father. He was not a demonstrative man and, though he did his best to look

235

after my physical needs, he did not talk a lot. When he did talk at all it was mostly about his work at the prison. I remember times when we sat together eating dinner at the kitchen table and he would tell me a little about the history of the prison.

"During the war the place was used to house Japanese prisoners of war, son," he told me. "A lot of them were creative. They created beautiful furniture and stunning artwork. A lot of these people were good farmers who reared their own beef, poultry and even vegetables. They clung to their skills and culture and I've been told they never gave up their hopes and dreams. The Japanese held on to their mysteries and didn't share them with anyone outside the prison."

"Were they our enemies, dad?"

"That's what we were told, son. But as far as I know they were just good people who tried to make a life for themselves even inside prison walls. I can tell you they were better than me, Jacob!"

"Better than you? Dad, why do you say that?"

"Because they never gave up!"

As a kid growing up I cherished these times when I would sit at the kitchen table with my father. It seemed that when he talked about these Japanese prisoners he was opening a door and letting me in; letting me feel, if only for a short time, close to him.

But these times were rare. Most of the time I felt alone and lonely. I wanted friends but I didn't seem to have the gift of knowing how to cultivate them. I guess to others I appeared to be as aloof as my father seemed to be with me. I would walk to school alone always with my seven stones in my pocket. Whenever I felt afraid I would put my hand into my pocket and allow the energy emanating from the special seven to flow through me.

Whenever a new stone captured my imagination I would pick it up, put it into my left trouser pocket. I would then thoughtfully choose which one from my right trouser pocket to be discarded. The choice was always a tough one to make. Once my decision was made I would make my way to the water's edge. There I would skip the chosen stone into oblivion.

Throughout the remainder of my elementary school days I lived with my father. He kept mostly to himself and I learned to do the same. I didn't know that my father was drinking too much alcohol. I thought drinking lots of beer was something that all fathers did. And the beer drinking never kept my father from going to the prison and doing his assigned tasks.

By the time I started high school my father started carrying a mickey of rye in the inside pocket of his jacket. I wasn't told the reason why but I think he was fired from his job at the prison because of his alcoholism. I did ask him once.

"Why did they let you go, dad?"

"Because they are fools, son," he told me. "You will discover that this world is full of fools."

My father always kept the fridge well stocked with beer. Because he was always high on whiskey he wasn't the best judge of how many beers he consumed. That's why he didn't miss the beers that I started to drink when I was fourteen.

Even though Dad wasn't working anymore he always seemed to have money to spend. I was just a kid and I didn't make it my business to know where the money was coming from.

By the time I was eighteen and in my last year of high school my father would give me the beer. The alcohol was a bond we shared, father and son. We would sit at the kitchen table and though my father was never sober I soon would be just as drunk as him.

I did my quiet drinking at night and never missed a day of school. When I was eighteen I graduated from high school. My grades were nothing to brag about but I was awarded my high school diploma.

Two weeks after graduation I came home as usual. My father was asleep on the couch. I didn't try to wake him. I was used to him passing out mid-morning, mid-day or half way through an evening. But when he didn't wake up after several hours I shook his shoulder,

"Hey dad, wake up!"

I was sort of on the drunk side of things myself when I realized my father was not going to wake up but I had enough sense to call 911. The doctor later told me my father died of cirrhosis of the liver, an illness caused by his prolonged alcohol abuse.

At the time of his death I had no job. I wasn't too concerned about money because I knew I would inherit my grandmother's house. My plan was to sell it but when I talked with the local lawyer I was informed that my father had taken out a big mortgage on the house. It was his borrowing that had kept the roof over our heads since he had been fired.

There was nothing material to inherit but the sins of the father were now mine to commit. I was just like Dad. Just like he had done I scraped up enough money to rent a room in the only rooming house in town. Unlike my father I used illegitimate ways to earn my income.

I became quite adept at break and enter. The stuff I stole was easily redeemed for cash at a pawnshop in Iroquois Falls. I also sold pharmaceuticals, the illegal kind, and soon had a good customer base in towns surrounding Monteith. I got my supplies from a more major dealer in Timmins. Before long I was able to develop a small client base in Timmins too.

I made a good income as a drug dealer. I never had any desire to partake of the drugs but by the time I was twenty-one I never had to reach far to get the mickey of rye out of my inside jacket pocket.

With no family and no facility for making friends I was what the psychologists would call a classic loner. I was drunk more often than sober. I became careless in my work, though I would have been the last to admit it. When the bust took place I was charged. In what seemed a very short time I was an inmate in the very prison that had kept my father employed all those years.

I was labeled an alcoholic. Being in Monteith Correctional Complex was not the worst thing that could have happened to me. It was a place where I could dry up and it provided me with some free rental space.

The worst part of being sent to Monteith was that upon my arrival the guards demanded I give up all my material possessions. I could care less about my wallet or any money it contained but when they demanded that I give up my seven stones I lost it.

I begged, "Please mister, they're just stupid stones. Please let me keep the damn stones?"

They would not.

After that I spent weeks in a fog. I didn't remember anything of the drying out process. I knew only that one morning I woke up with a clear head. The clarity scared me.

During this time of incarceration in Monteith Correctional Complex an old barn on the prison grounds was to be torn down. My first job at the prison was my first legitimate job since graduation. I assisted in taking up the barn boards from the hayloft floor. I was in the process of pulling off a floor board when I found a small faded white cotton bag the top hem of which contained a dirty white piece of ordinary string. The string was tied in a loose bow.

I was working under the scrutiny of a prison guard and, of course, I was not the only worker taking that hayloft floor apart. When I spotted the little bag, though my curiosity was at its height, I did nothing. I worked as usual. When I was convinced no one was paying the slightest attention to me in one swift movement of my right hand I swept up the little bag. Raising my right arm in a pretense of scratching my head I felt the bag make its way up my sleeve. There the bag remained while with extreme care I continued to work. Holding my arm close to my body I ensured its safe keeping until finally I was alone back in my jail cell.

It was not until that evening that I felt secure enough to loosen the string and look inside the bag. I saw seven small flat stones. At once I felt the connection to my past, my future and my forgotten connection to the God I had met years before in the Baptist Church where Grandma Ellie had sent me to learn the story of Jacob's ladder.

Finding these seven stones was a mystical experience that would transform my life. I could see that the stones each were transcribed with Japanese calligraphy. This discovery made me feel very close to my father. I remembered sitting at the kitchen table with my Dad while he told me all about the Japanese prisoners of war.

The fact that there were exactly seven stones was, to me, miraculous. Since my Grandma's death until my more recent incarceration I had always carried seven stones in my pocket. Somehow I knew that these seven stones connected me to my mother, my grandmother and to God. These stones were my Jacob's ladder and now this ladder was in my possession again.

There was no doubt in my mind that these seven stones were the bridge between my past, my future; my life on earth and my heavenly connection.

I treasured these flat stones. Throughout the years of my imprisonment I rarely removed them from their safe hiding place. Just knowing they were there was enough.

Each of these stones contained Japanese calligraphy. I wanted to know what the symbols meant.

I borrowed book after book from the prison library but I was never able to find an answer to this mystery.

I was twenty-four when I was finally released from prison. I was clean and sober. With the aid of government social workers, I made my way to Toronto where I found work with a contracting firm. I followed the advice of my probation officer and ensured that my employer knew of my past criminal record. For the first time since Gram's death I was beginning to feel some purpose in my life.

Each day I carried the seven stones in my right trouser pocket. At night when I went to bed I placed one stone under my pillow while the other six rested on my bedside table.

Unlike the tearing up of floorboards I did at Monteith, in my new job I assisted with the laying of hardwood floors in a large city apartment building under construction. I was one of many workers on the job.

This day a fellow employee approached me as I was leaving the jobsite to take my coffee break. He introduced himself as Yamado.

"Hi, Yamado. I'm Jacob."

As I caressed the seven flat stones in my pocket I could not resist the urge to ask him. "Yamado, are you Japanese?"

"I'm Canadian."

"Yeah, sure, okay," I said knowing I had over-stepped a boundary.

Yamado laughed. "It is okay, Jacob. I'm proud to be Japanese-Canadian."

I invited him to sit with me while we had our coffee break. While we relaxed at the cafeteria table I raised enough courage to ask, "Yamado, do you know anything about Japanese calligraphy?"

"No," he replied. "Nothing."

I guess I was visibly disappointed because he then smiled and said, "My sister studied Japanese calligraphy in college."

I could not believe my good fortune. I reached into my pocket and for the first time in my life I shared a stone collection. Yamado was impressed and we made a date for that evening to meet with his sister.

As I made my way toward his home that night I fondled the seven flat stones in my pocket. I knocked on his apartment door with anticipation.

Yamado opened the door and with outstretched hand he said, "Jacob, welcome to my home."

"Thanks for inviting me, Yamado."

He led me into his living room. There, seated on the sofa, was a most beautiful young Japanese woman.

"Jacob, meet my sister, Izanagi Taro."

I held her outstretched hand. Warm energy flowed throughout my body.

"It's a pleasure to meet you, Izanagi. You have a very interesting name."

Yamato jumped in and said, "Izanagi means female who invites."

We all laughed and as I removed the cotton bag containing the flat stones from my pocket, I responded, "Izanagi, thank you for inviting me and for offering to translate the calligraphy on these stones."

I handed the dirty, faded bag to Izanagi who removed the stones and spread them out on her brother's coffee table. She moved them about until she appeared satisfied with their order of placement on the table's surface. Then looking up at me she spoke.

"You may be disappointed, Jacob. Each marking is simply a letter from the alphabet."

I did feel let down a little. "What are the letters, Izanagi?" I asked.

"I've placed them in alphabetical order, Jacob. They are the letters A, H, J, M, S, T and Y. Do they hold special meaning for you?"

"Not at all."

"Could it be an anagram?" Yamado suggested. "If you rearranged the letters would they form a word that holds special meaning?"

"What a great idea!" I exclaimed. "But how will I know which letter is which when I cannot read the calligraphy?"

"I will take care of that for you," Izanagi offered. She proceeded to write the English letters onto a page of computer paper. She then cut the sheet of paper into squares each containing a letter. With scotch tape she attached the written English letter onto the appropriate flat stone."

"Thank you, Izanagi."

"You are most welcome, Jacob. While you get to work I will make us all some tea," she offered.

Yamado watched as I played with the flat stones. I came up with My Hats with a J left over.

Yamado took a turn. "Perhaps it is someone's name," he said as he spelled out J.M. Hasty.

This was a big challenge. I spelled out Jyst Ham.

"Jyst ham?" Yamado laughed. "What is that?"

"I have no idea."

Just then Izanagi returned to the room with a tray containing three steaming cups of green tea and a platter of sandwiches.

"Can we make room on the coffee table for this tray?" she asked.

"Of course," Yamado replied.

I took a bite of one of the sandwiches. "Delicious! Izanagi, what kind of sandwich is this?"

"It's just ham," she answered.

"What did you say?" Yamado shouted.

"Why are you shouting, Yamado? I said it's just ham for goodness sakes."

"Just ham!"

"Just ham? Jyst ham?" Then I could not contain my laughter.

"Hey guys, let me in on the joke! What's so darn funny about ham sandwiches?" Izanagi insisted.

"Look at the stones, Izanagi," her brother laughed.

She did. "Oh, no, it's not possible!" And she was laughing too.

The mystery of the stones is a secret well-kept by the Japanese prisoner of war who buried the small cotton bag beneath the floor boards of the hayloft. I never did find out the true meaning behind the Japanese calligraphy letters on my flat stones but somehow, after that evening in Yamado's apartment, it didn't matter.

These seven letters would always hold special meaning to me. They were Jacob's ladder indeed. They were my stairway to Heaven because they had led me to a meeting with Izanagi Taro.

In time I married this beautiful woman. In all our years together I never once touched a drop of alcohol. Always I carried my seven stones in my trouser pocket. Izanagi and I grew old together. The day of my retirement from the construction industry came and soon after we sold our Toronto home and moved to Monteith where I built us a home on the very spot where my Grandma Ellie's little old house once sat.

I am back home at last. I am at peace.

When I die I will climb Jacob's ladder to be with my grandmother, my parents and one day I know I will be joined by my loving wife, Izanagi. In my Last Will and Testament I have requested someone to take the seven stones where they can be skipped into the Abitibi River. They have served me well throughout my life and that is where they belong. Because of the seven stones I found the strength to break the cycle of alcoholism and self-abuse. Like the Japanese prisoners of war, I never gave up.

About the Author:

Audrey Austin was born and raised by her parents in Toronto, Ontario, Canada. At an early age she married and before long her two daughters arrived. Having only a high school education she waited until her children were grown before going back to school. She attended University of Toronto and later graduated from Transformational Arts College. She has lived in Toronto & its suburbs; Prince Edward Island and in New Zealand. She has enjoyed other international travel but only as a tourist in countries such as Thailand; Korea; Bahamas; Bermuda; Columbia, Puno and Cartagena in South America.

She always wanted to write and did so in a small way as a hobby but never made any attempt at publication. It was not until she retired at an uncertain age that she finally made the promise to herself that she would fulfill her dream of being an author. She loves creative writing and how can something one loves so much be classified as work? She has written novels, novellas, and short stories always doing her best to keep up with the characters. Audrey is currently living in Elliot Lake, Ontario, Canada.

http://www.amazon.com/author/audreyaustin

http://www.facebook.com/audreyaustinca

www.ingramcontent.com/pod-product-compliance
Lightning Source LLC
Chambersburg PA
CBHW051148030726
47504CB00004B/1095